Moondust

By Nei

Dedication

To my wonderful wife Jifelane, for her patience and support through the marathon that producing this book has been. Thanks too, to all the children who've listened to or read the unpolished version of Moondust and given helpful feedback – you are stars!

Chapter 1

The empty clang of the old grandfather clock in the hall at Fern Cottage pierced the lingering silence. It chimed eight times. I yawned, dangled my legs over the edge of the bed and gazed out of the window to admire the final crimson glow of the setting sun. Like a stalking cat, darkness had crept over the horizon. I lifted my legs back on to the bed, curled up and closed my eyes. Slowly, I drifted into a daydream and lost myself in my imagination. Without warning, the fierce roar of a mighty metallic beast burst through my half opened window. I sprang up as it cut through the comfort of my thoughts. The noise lasted for an ear splitting moment before drifting back out of the room. The beast grunted past and rumbled further into the night. Wandering tractors sometimes brought a glimmer of excitement to this sleepy part of the world. I scrambled off my bed, flung the door open and called downstairs.

"Dad, can I stargaze tonight?"

"Have you finished your homework?"

"Not yet."

"You need to finish it before you can go out."

"Why can't I do it later?"

"You know the rules."

"Yeah, yeah, your rules," I muttered quietly.

"I'm nearly finished," I shouted, and pulled my school books out of my old brown leather satchel.

Dad's voice thundered up the stairs again. "Hurry up or you won't have time. And stop daydreaming. When you're done you can have half an hour."

He knew me too well. I was always daydreaming. I could have finished my homework ages before.

I copied the spellings I needed to learn and tested myself. I sniffed, rubbed my nose and lay back down on my bed.

Every boy has a crazy dream. Mine was to be the daredevil captain of an indestructible spaceship on a mission to discover planets not yet named. I wanted to fly faster than a shooting star, steer towards Saturn and smash through her frozen ice rings like a mighty missile. Desperate for adventure, I dreamed of zooming out of our solar system to explore the deep silent space beyond.

I fed my crazy dream gazing at the stars. Whenever the skies were still and clear, I would lie under the majesty of the night sky, a darkness shimmering with light from every corner of the universe. I loved to let my imagination run wild. Although the stars were distant beyond measure, I felt part of them. To me, the stars were more than giant fiery masses of burning gas. It was like I knew them and they knew me. The stars were my friends.

I shoved my books back into my satchel and ran downstairs. Dressed in thick blue jeans, a warm sweater and pale brown duffle coat, I flicked the switch for the kitchen light and rubbing my hands together I headed towards my favourite spot in the garden with Dad's old grey blanket and my goose down pillow tucked under my arm. The spring air was still and a few small, wispy clouds drifted overhead. The scent of freshly cut grass tickled my nostrils. My nose itched like mad and before I could scratch it, a gigantic sneeze exploded out of my mouth.

I knelt down and rolled out the blanket. Placing the pillow, I stretched out and wriggled to get comfortable.

Fern cottage was about a mile west of the small Shropshire town of Church Stretton and in a perfect place for studying the night sky. We had a clear view in three directions.

I squinted several times. Slowly my eyes became more accustomed to the darkness and the night sky unfolded. I studied the heavens with the watchfulness of a starving eagle hovering over its prey. With only the bleating of distant sheep for company I gazed in wonder. Blue Giant, Red Dwarf and Super Nova stars flickered into view. The more I studied the more I saw. I picked out The Plough and The Little Bear star formations.

My favourite formation was Orion the hunter. As I found it, my thoughts wandered as I imagined Orion the hunter as some kind of galactic superhero. I pictured a mighty space warrior wielding his dazzling sword - a slicing, cutting silver blade of death. It flashed like demented fork lightning back and forth across the galaxy. He smashed it into a distant sun, piercing it through to its fiery heart. Like a cosmic firework show, the star exploded into billions of pieces, sending tiny balls of burning gas drifting further into deep space.

I sucked my breath in deeply several times filling my lungs and as I released it I watched it quickly melt into the night. In the stillness, my thoughts turned to fond memories of *Hogan,* our wonderful old Red Setter who had died two weeks after Christmas. I thought about him often. He had been in the family forever and the cottage was empty without him. Now I carried a tiny rust coloured shooting star in my pocket to remember him. Dad found it while walking on the moor back in February. As I rolled it in my hands, the spiky edges pressed in and made my skin tingle. It was heavier than a large marble and shimmered with the rugged beauty of something that had burned and hurtled through space for millions of miles.

As I continued to gaze into the night it was like someone was turning all the lights on. More stars appeared as my eyes continued to adjust. I gripped my blanket and wrapped it around me as I felt the chill. My thoughts wandered again. What an amazing year 1969 had been so far in 'The Space Race.' The two world 'superpower' countries, the USA and the USSR, were like two giant heavyweight boxers, pouring sweat and landing power packed punches on each other. Standing toe to toe, they slugged out space achievements for all they were worth...

THUD! January 16th Soyuz Four and Five of the USSR were the first two manned spacecraft to dock in space.

BAMM! Later in March, Apollo Nine of the USA performed the first manned flight of a lunar module.

SLAM! My thoughts were interrupted as the kitchen door thudded to a close. Mum approached. Her familiar footsteps crunched through the grass, spraying small drops of evening dew in every direction. The crisp air had already grabbed my feet and wrapped them in its icy grip. My half hour had flown and it was time for bed.

“Eddiebies!” she called, in a high pitched voice.

Why didn’t she say ‘time for bed’ like most mums do? I didn’t move. Ignoring her had worked before.

Her voice softened.

“Come on Edward Frost, you’ve got a big day tomorrow.”

It was one more sleep ‘til my birthday but I wasn’t ready for bed.

“Five more minutes ... please.”

“No, you’ve had enough.”

“That’s what you think,” I grumbled.

Her footsteps softly crunched the ground behind me and she waited as I lay there determined to squeeze in the last possible drop of time. Then she stepped forward, stood as still as a post box and leaned over me. Her arms were folded and her eyes were narrowed.

“There’s a big fat spider on your pillow!” she whispered.

That was the moment I panicked and like a deranged grasshopper I sprang into action, shaking my head, my shoulders and my arms.

“Ha-ha! Gotcha!” she chuckled. I can’t believe I fell for that one again. Tricked out of an extra few minutes I trudged back to the house.

“Go sort yourself out for bed and I’ll be up in a few minutes to tuck you in.”

It didn't take me long to get ready. Mum and Dad came into my room together to say goodnight. After lights out I lay awake dreaming about the day ahead ... presents, gooey chocolate birthday cake and playing my favourite game in the garden... crab football! But from out of nowhere my peaceful bliss was broken. Two short heart-stopping words had popped into my head ... RAT FACE. Thinking about him was like stumbling across an unexploded bomb. His real name was John Anderson and he was the last of the dreaded Anderson brothers to go through my school. Pure and simple, he was a bully. He took after his older brothers and made everyone's life at school a misery *and* he was in *my* class. Even on normal days he would steal and hide your pencils and marbles, scribble on your exercise books and call you all the names you hated. Another of his 'jokes' was tying your laces together and sticking chewing gum to your hair. Outside he would sneak up from behind, trip you over and stand over you laughing. He had regular trips to see old Mr Crenshaw, the head teacher at our school. But none of these visits ever seemed to put him off. He was relentless. However, it was on your birthday that he would give you special attention – 'Johnny's b-b-birthday surprise' he called it, always with his slightly embarrassing stutter. If he knew it was your birthday he would make your day a miserable one. He was the birthday spoiler. Tomorrow would probably be my turn.

I took ages to get to sleep. I twisted and squirmed around in bed like a maggot in a fisherman's bait box, my throat became dry and I reached for the comfort of my shooting star. This time it didn't help. Worries grew into murky menacing monsters. Every sound was magnified and every thought sent me spinning deeper into the dungeon of dreadful dreams.

Chapter 2

The air in my bedroom was thick with the salty whiff of fried bacon. Drifting up from the kitchen it had tickled my nostrils and woken the taste making factory in my mouth.

"Ed, breakfast!"

Mum's voice was comforting after my late night scary thoughts. I threw back the blanket, jumped out of bed and hurtled down the stairs. I somehow avoided falling head first, legged it down the hallway and flung the kitchen door wide open.

"HAPPY BIRTHDAY!" exclaimed Mum and Dad together. Great big smiles stretched across their excited faces.

I froze in the doorway, hands on hips. In front of me was a birthday present I had not dared to dream of. Mounted on an oak tripod and glinting proudly in the morning sun was a *Jason Empire* telescope!

Dad spoke first.

"Now you can dream to your heart's content."

Why did he always have to poke fun at my daydreaming?

I scratched my head and muttered a very happy ‘thank you’. I ran my fingers over the cold metal of the long tube before pressing my right eye to the lens of the telescope. This was going to be incredible. Now I could *really* star gaze.

The next half hour was a bit of a blur. After devouring Mum’s delicious fried breakfast the only thing I remember is opening some of my birthday cards. There was one from Grandma and Grandpa Frost all the way from Seattle, USA. By ‘coincidence’ it had a telescope on the front. I stuffed the card into my school bag eager to show off to my friends.

I washed, dressed and finally set off for school. Mum gave me the usual embarrassing kiss on the cheek. Dad put his hand on my shoulder and we exchanged big smiles. I jogged the half mile down Burmill Lane in no time, desperate to tell my mate Bertie all about the *Jason Empire*.

Bertie Jones was my best friend. We all called him ‘rubber chops’. Once, I saw him at the back of a morning assembly squeeze a whole tennis ball in his mouth. Bertie was also clever, sharp like a new razorblade. He had an answer for everything, which sometimes got him in trouble. Bertie was in the year above me at school. He was brilliant at sport and even more brilliant at pulling freaky faces. He had a mop of brown curly hair, a few freckles and a cheeky face to go with it. He was waiting at the end of the lane, leaning up against a gatepost.

"You're late."

I checked my watch as I continued to walk towards him. He was right but only by a few minutes. Today I had a good excuse anyway.

"What's that face all about?" he asked. "You've got a smile like a sliced watermelon." He stretched his mouth into a massively exaggerated grin.

As we headed for school in the bright morning sunshine I told him all about my brilliant birthday surprise. We arrived in no time.

"Nice one Ed," said Bertie on the way to our class lines. "Maybe we can spot the Martians invading."

Our school, Edgerton Junior, was a busy little school. The teachers were caring and thoughtful enough except for Mr Smedley who always seemed so serious. 'Smiler' we called him. You could hear his ranting and raving from one end of school to the other. Old Mr Crenshaw the Headmaster was a bit different too. He was a tall, mysterious figure who seldom came out of his office.

'CLANG! CLANG! CLANG!' the tinny old school bell brought everyone scurrying to their class lines. Bossy prefects with their little red badges took turns to ring it each morning. The teachers appeared, tea mugs in hand and marched us off to our classes.

Miss Taylor was my teacher. She was tall, wore round-rimmed glasses and had jet black curly hair with a streak of red. Her clothes were always colourful. She lit up our dull classroom with her long flowery pink, yellow and purple skirts. Heavy-scented lemon perfume wafted in the air around her. Bertie called her hippy Taylor. He said that if she became fat he would call her Hippytaylormus. I liked her. She never raised her voice and last Christmas she bought everyone in the class an Aztec chocolate bar*.

The first lesson was Maths and I completed less than half a page of fractions. I kept looking over to where Rat Face was slouched in his chair.

He was across the room pulling foul faces. They were all aimed at me. He stared straight at me and mouthed the words 'You're in for it.' My brain got into a spin. Once Rat Face started to pick on you he was like a crocodile with a fresh meal in its jaws. Miss Taylor gave me one of her teacher stares. Realising I had started to sniff, I pinched my nose desperate to act as normally as I could.

As my thoughts wandered to what might happen at break time my fears got worse. Rat Face would seek you out like some guided nuclear missile. He was good at sneaking under the teacher's radar too and nobody grassed him up, ever. Nobody ever dared. My stomach churned like a cement mixer spinning out of control. A pencil flying from John's direction whizzed past my ear, almost jabbing Miss Taylor's foot. Amazingly, she was so busy talking she didn't notice. Rat Face kept staring at me. The skilful hunter was stalking its terrified prey and today it was me.

With his black spiky hair and toothy grin, John Anderson looked remarkably like 'Deathshead' Danny Morgan from Beano's Bash Street Kids. Some kids called him Danny to try and get his respect but he didn't much care. Most kids stuck to calling him Rat Face behind his back and from a very safe distance. His parents, Alfie and Marge, ran a scrap metal dealer place. According to our local newspaper the *Shropshire Star*, they had been fined several times for receiving stolen goods. All the local Bobbies knew the Andersons.

Nobody at school liked Rat Face. He had no real friends and liked his own company. Everyone avoided him. No one wanted trouble. My stomach continued to churn. The joy of my brilliant birthday surprise had faded and as morning break approached and with every fiendish face he pulled, I dreaded what Rat Face might get up to.

Break soon arrived and as I put my books in my desk I could see bully boy smirking and glaring at me from across the class before disappearing down the corridor. I lingered near Miss Taylor's desk, pretending I needed to talk about maths but she grabbed some workbooks without noticing me and scurried off. I made my way out of the classroom and slipped my duffle coat on, taking as much time as I could. As I ambled along the corridor towards the playground, stopping to untie and tie my laces, I felt so alone. I hoped Bertie would be outside but I remembered that his class had gone up the hill to do some sketching. I stepped out onto the playground and could see all my friends in the distance, playing across the other side of the field. Duty teachers were nowhere to be seen and the early morning sunlight was lost behind the gathering clouds. I stood on my own and trembled as I realised my moment had come.

"Hey b-birthday boy, I wonder what's in here then?"

I glanced across the playground. Rat Face had snatched my school bag off my peg and was rummaging through the contents. That sly grin seemed forever stuck to his annoying face.

I was now becoming Rat Face's latest victim. Forced into playing his miserable little bully game I reached into my pocket and gripped my lucky space rock hoping for even a grain of courage. I felt helpless, locked into something I wanted no part of. I sniffed loudly, bit my lip and hoped that someone would notice my emergency. No one did. But then something snapped in my head and I was filled with a foolish kind of bravery. I took one small step towards him and looked straight into his eyes. I was going to at least try to get my bag back.

"Leave it bully boy!" I shouted. Too late, he had pulled out the birthday card from grandma and grandpa. He dropped the bag and sprinted off, waving the card in the air and celebrating like he'd scored the winning goal in the cup final.

"Come and get it, J-J-Jack," he taunted. I hated being called Jack Frost and he knew it.

Furious and foolishly unafraid I raced towards him. Now I wanted to play. Now I'd let him have his little game. If he wanted to play then so did I. Deliberately, Rat Face stopped and held the card above my head, knowing I wouldn't be able to reach it. I stretched up and felt like a right idiot waving my arm around in thin air. But the foolish bravery was still with me. I continued to hold my shooting star.

"What a stupid c-c-card! A stupid card for a stupid boy! Ooooh and it's from Grandma and Grandpa Frost. Where do they live, the North P-Pole?"

My craziness turned into a fuming flurry. I became like a Grizzly Bear whose food had just been stolen. Out of nowhere came a crazy idea, really crazy, but I went for it all the same. I was ready to do something no one had ever dared to do to Rat Face before…operation tickle whizzed into action! 'SHTUNNG!' my arm sprung into action. 'Flick, flap!' I reached up under John's freckled chin and … 'jiggajiggajigga!' I tickled him on his dirty little neck. I couldn't believe it! He wriggled and squirmed like a piglet in the mud. He had no idea how to fight back. This was unbelievable ... me, teasing Rat Face. The tickle attack was working. Now he was *my* prisoner in *my* little game. My fears had melted like ice under a giant's sweaty armpit. Rat Face was helpless under a shower of tickles and beginning to taste some of his own medicine.

"Eeeek!" he squealed and started to giggle like a baby, dropping the card in a flash. Julie Pearson saw what happened. She sprinted over to join in the tickle attack and aimed a delighted finger at his ribs. 'Kerjink!!' He squirmed again, desperate to evade another tickling shot. Too late, Julie aimed a second powerful tickle poke under his arm. John Anderson's power relied on scare tactics and now all that power was evaporating. This was momentous! Our tickle jabs rained in on him from all directions.

Next, little Basil Scott appeared and chipped in. He went for the side of the neck. Basil being brave … this was a first! His tickle hand swished through the air … 'eeeeeooowwww prang!' Jackpot! Rat Face was a blubbering mess.

"Eeeheeeheeeee! Oooohaha! Heeeheee! St-st-sto-o-o-p!" yelled Rat Face. He looked and sounded ridiculous. Doubled up and defenceless he was like a mental monkey as we continued to jab and prod him. There was no sympathy for the bully. A bit of a crowd gathered. They saw what was happening and stood round laughing and pointing. Bully boy was completely embarrassed and a defeated foe, beaten by tickles. What would his 'Ma' and 'Pa' think of him now? 'Smiler' approached without us noticing.

"Break it up right now!" he exploded. I jumped and froze as he grabbed me by the arm. Basil and Julie stepped away. Rat Face's lower lip quivered and his eyes welled up. He lost control and burst into tears.

At that moment, the bell rang. 'Smiler' seemed in a bit of a hurry and after making Rat Face apologise for taking my card and bag, he sent us to our line. George 'maggot' Maggs was in front of me. He was the most annoying boy in the class, a tell tale and a show off. He turned around, pointed and sniggered.

"You're for it 'Jack Frost'," he said.

Still fuming, I wanted to wipe that annoying smirk off his face.

As we made our way back to class, Smiler reappeared and pointed to Rat Face and me.

"You two, go to Mr Crenshaw's office... now!"

Mr Crenshaw only ever appeared for assemblies, parents meetings and the occasional rugby sevens match. He wore a long black gown which swirled in time with his footsteps. His low, dreary voice was more frightening than Smiler's and his cold blue eyes often drilled straight through you. I was terrified and although Rat Face had seen him many times before, he was now going to Crenshaw's office in defeat.

I tapped on the door. There was a long pause.

"Come," his deep voice filled me with terror. The sniffs came back.

I pushed down the old brass handle and the newly painted shiny black door slowly creaked open. We inched forward. The dimly lit room smelled of wood polish. With his piercing eyes Mr Crenshaw pinned us to the spot in front of his desk. He sat forward, arms folded. We bowed our heads like we were ready to pray.

"Bullying again were you Anderson?"

"Sir."

"Speak up boy, I can't hear you. And take your hands out of your pockets."

Rat Face cleared his throat and glanced up before bowing his head again.

"Yes, s-sir."

"And you Frost, why are you here?"

Memories of the tickle attack were fresh and vivid. I couldn't believe what I was about to say to old Mr Crenshaw but I could feel the giggles coming and nothing could stop them.

"Tickling, sir."

I was desperate not to laugh but completely lost it. For what seemed an age I giggled out of control. My head was down, my shoulders shook violently and my hands tried to cover my face. It just seemed funny, that's all. Since when was tickling a crime? In the end I had the courage to look up and Crenshaw's icy look brought me to my senses. Before bowing my head again I thought I saw a tiny smirk on Crenshaw's face. I glimpsed over at 'Rat Face.' There were tears in his eyes again.

"Sorry, sir," I said, looking up again for a moment.

"I should jolly well think so, Frost. Anderson, I hope you've learnt your lesson."

"Sir."

The 'hang dog' look on his face said it all. His bully balloon had been well and truly popped.

"I'll be phoning your Pa, Anderson."

He hung his head even lower.

"Frost, I'll be phoning your mother. Get out both of you."

We trudged back to class without a word or a glance. I began to think that mum might cancel my birthday party. She would be so disappointed. What started as such an amazing day had turned into a disaster. Grasping my lucky space rock in my sweaty palm I wished that the day would get better. Instead, as I arrived back in class everyone stared, Miss Taylor ignored me and Maggot managed another annoying little smirk. I clung on to my little shooting star. Rat Face wiped the tears from his eyes.

I tried to turn my thoughts back to my wonderful telescope and capture the excitement I had felt earlier. Why should Rat Face spoil my day? But it was too late; I couldn't stop thinking about the mess I was in.

To make things worse, before he shuffled into his seat, Rat Face sneered and whispered, "I'm going to tell my b-b-big brother Tony all about you."

As my stomach tightened I swallowed hard and looked down at the tiled floor. For a brief moment I felt the dread of the previous night, before comforting myself with the thought of Rat Face blubbering out of control in Crenshaw's office.

Chapter 3

Worried about losing my party and still fuming about my unfair visit to old Mr Crenshaw's office, I sneaked into the dimly lit kitchen. The windows at Fern Cottage were small and the rooms were poorly lit even on sunny days. Thin lines of sunlight creeping through the gaps in Mum's new blinds were just enough to light my way. As I trudged towards the living room I could hear the dull tick of the large clock hanging on the wall. I threw my satchel on the kitchen table, hung up my duffle coat and went to find Mum. She was sat on the sofa calmly sipping a cup of tea. I took a quiet sniff and pressed myself up behind an armchair. Mum put down her cup, stared up at me and the battle of words began.

"Old Mr Crenshaw was so disappointed. 'Let down' were the exact words he used."

So Crenshaw *had* kept his promise.

"But he didn't even bother to find out what happened," I grumbled.

"*I* feel let down too – *and* on your birthday." Mum sank deeper into the sofa and took another sip of tea.

"Aren't *you* going to bother to find out what happened, either?" I said.

All mum cared about was being 'let down'.

I clenched my fist and thumped the back of the chair. It wasn't my fault and mum was clueless about what really happened. She looked straight into my eyes and ignored my little outburst.

"I'm sure Mr Crenshaw knows more than you think. He's a wily old fox."

"So what did he say?" I said.

"You and some friends were picking on John Anderson."

What? I couldn't believe what I was hearing. Rat Face was the one picking on *me*. I was defending myself and trying to get my birthday card back.

"But that's not all that happened. Before break ..."

Mum interrupted me.

"... *and* you made John Anderson cry."

"Mum, listen! Can I just..."

Before I could have my say she cut me short again. This was getting ridiculous.

"Mr Crenshaw also told me that John had been teasing you and had taken your birthday card. He told me you had used the latest tickle technology to fight back."

So there *was* a tiny smirk on his face. Crenshaw was human after all.

As she got up to go to the kitchen, mum beamed a broad 'knowing' smile. She spoke as she ambled across the room.

"I'm disappointed you had to go to Mr Crenshaw's office, but so proud that you stood up for yourself. That must have been a hard thing to do."

I sighed, wishing I hadn't interrupted her in the first place.

Mum opened the kitchen door wide and the sweet aroma of baked chocolate cake drifted towards me. It was like honey, vanilla and cocoa all mixed into one. I was going to get my birthday party after all.

Later that evening, Mum's cake was a massive hit with all my friends. We devoured every crumb. Basil looked like he'd grown a moustache with blobs of chocolate icing stuck all around the top of his mouth. We played games in the garden and chatted about what happened with 'Rat Face'. I was a bit embarrassed really, as it was something I did in the heat of the moment and it could have turned out a disaster.

Everyone left by eight thirty. Happy, tired and with my mind spinning with the events of the day, I was in bed by nine o'clock. Although I tried to wait patiently for Dad I must have drifted off to sleep. When he brought the radio up he had to dig me in the ribs to wake me. He had promised we could listen to a special programme. When I opened my eyes, however, the first thing I noticed was raised eyebrows and a hard stare.

"I bumped into Peter Maggs in the newsagents. Told me all about what happened with you and John Anderson at school. Said George saw it all." Dad folded his arms.

That was a lie for a start - typical Maggot. George Maggs was always blabbering. Dad had heard only half the story.

Before Dad could lecture me any further I jumped in and explained the whole drama. He soon changed his mind.

"Well done son, I think the bully might have learnt his lesson."

"I wish you'd talked to Mum first. She could have told you what happened."

Dad apologised.

The special programme on the new Radio Four was all about the plans for the first ever moon landing coming up in July. It was mind boggling but I loved it. Maybe my dream *was* possible. Dad laughed. The name of one of the astronauts fascinated me too – Buzz Aldrin. 'Excellent name,' I thought, 'sounds like a super hero!' As Dad strolled out of the room my thoughts drifted once again and I set my heart on warm summer evenings under the stars with my new telescope, gazing into deep space, dreaming of adventures on those planets not yet named.

Chapter 4

Thwack! Dad flung open my bedroom door and it thudded against the painted stone wall, jolting me from my unbroken sleep. The floorboards creaked as Dad's heavy footsteps thumped against them. He strode further into my room and threw back the curtains. The morning sunlight blazed in and I squinted as I tried to shield my eyes.

"Time to get up son," he blurted, right next to my ear.

Dad often had to drag me out of bed on Saturdays to do my chores. Sweeping the kitchen, dusting the shelves and helping Dad clean his car were my usual duties. He was used to me diving under the bed sheet to delay them, so today his large hand gripped my shoulder and gave me a firm shake. Doing chores often gave me the grumps, but today was different. The sooner I got them done, the sooner I could use my wonderful new telescope. So I rolled out of bed, grabbed a bowl of cereal and got started.

Dad had agreed to set up the *Jason* in the garden once I had finished today's tasks – cleaning the car and cutting the grass. I couldn't wait. By lunchtime I was as excited as a hungry shark watching a fat pirate walk the plank.

Over hot creamy tomato soup, with crunchy bread rolls and butter, Dad tried without success to explain all the extra pieces of equipment that came with the telescope. Truth was I was too distracted to listen. I'd find out how they worked later. With the tang of the tomato still teasing my taste buds I raced ahead of him into the garden.

The sheep were bleating down in the valley and a lonely light aircraft droned overhead. The hazy spring sun warmed my face and lit up the hills and farmland on the horizon. Between us, Dad and I managed to set up the *Jason*. Dad disappeared back into the cottage and I adjusted the legs of the tripod, preparing the angle of the telescope for the evening star gaze. I sat still on the ground and looked up to admire the *Jason*. It stood proud glinting in the sunlight. Then came one of those moments when I couldn't help myself. I was itching to use my wonderful new gift so I rolled up my sleeves and changed the angle of the telescope to have a quick look at the landscape in the distance.

To begin with everything seemed to wobble. It was blurry and hard to focus. After a short while I got the hang of looking through the lens and the countryside in the distance came clearly into view. Bracken covered hills, trees, and rocky crags stuck up everywhere.

'Huh?' My whole body flinched. I hesitated, swallowed hard and sucked in a deep breath. Was that something moving between the trees? 'Must be the telescope wobble'. I looked a second time and froze as the object caught my eye again. I stared, my eye glued to the telescope. It was a tall, dark shape striding hastily across the heathland. An icy chill ran through me and my hand began to tremble. I began to make out a person striding along one of the many paths that criss-crossed the area. I followed the mystery figure as closely as I could.

'Just a Saturday walker,' I thought, trying to stay calm. Instinct told me to keep track of the mysterious hiker. I took another deep breath. As he walked through a clearing I could make out a man, wearing a dark overcoat and cap. Moving the telescope with my eye fixed to the lens was tricky but I persevered. He appeared to be carrying some kind of bag. Without warning he stopped, bent down for a moment then turned around. He looked up briefly and started back the way he came.

My heart was racing. I tracked him for another minute or so but he was going faster and was even more difficult to follow. Minutes later he disappeared from view behind a clump of trees. I adjusted the telescope again and tried to catch another glimpse of the stranger. But that was it – he'd gone.

I tried to stop my hands from trembling by gripping the tripod. As I did, I paused to reflect. Who was the mystery man? What was he carrying? Why did he carry something into such a remote place and appear to leave it behind? I replayed the scene over and over in my mind.

Should I go to the heathland and investigate? Although I knew more or less where the man had been, it would be almost impossible to find anything. There were so many places to look and the gorse bushes and rocky ground would make it tiring work. It was a long way to walk for what would probably be a bag of old rubbish. I couldn't tell Mum and Dad why I was going either. I tried to put what I had seen to the back of my mind, trying to convince myself that it didn't matter. I could help Dad with a spot of gardening and earn some pocket money. I went to the kitchen, poured myself a drink of cold lemonade and scratching my head I weighed up what I should do.

There had to be a sensible explanation for the stranger on the moor but as much as I tried, there was no logical answer I could think of. Something wasn't quite right. It was such an odd thing to see. My mind was flooded with questions and I *had* to dig deeper. Right then I made up my mind to head for the moor and play detective. It was a mystery I couldn't leave alone.

"Dad, can I phone Bertie?"

"Of course, you two got something planned?"

"Not really, just thought it would be nice to go for a bit of a hike."

I needed to hide the truth. What my parents didn't know couldn't hurt.

Over the phone I asked Bertie to come for a hike. I wanted to wait to tell him face to face what I had seen with the telescope.

“Be back by six,” Mum called down the stairs. I felt bad. Mum and Dad had always taught me not to lie to them, so now even a tiny lie felt huge. However, the temptation to discover what the mystery stranger had left behind was just too strong.

I put on my walking boots and anorak. Still pondering what I had let myself in for, I slipped out of the kitchen door. There was no turning back.

Chapter 5

As I stepped outside, the ice cold blast of the spring breeze covered my face. A shiver shuddered down my spine. I blew into my hands and rubbed them together. The sun was out but the breeze was blocking its heat.

I adjusted the strap on my rucksack and set off, desperate to find the object left by the mystery man. The small canvas rucksack on my back contained some useful supplies. Mum had insisted I take them. She had made a cheddar cheese and tomato sandwich, packed a water bottle, a Granny Smith apple and a bright red jumper that Grandma Frost had knitted last Christmas.

Another stray thought bothered me. Was I putting myself and Bertie in danger? A lonely blackbird scurried under the hedge distracting my attention. I slipped my hands into my pockets.

Bertie was already at the end of the lane, usual big grin on his face. He leaned against a gatepost and nodded in my direction as he tapped his foot.

"How's the telescope?" Bertie quizzed.

“Funny you should say that.” I told him everything I’d seen. Bertie looked at me and frowned.

“Love the sense of adventure,” he said, “but it’s got to be someone dumping rubbish.”

“It’s a long way to go to do that,” I said, walking ahead a bit faster. “There were plenty of better places he could have gone.”

Bertie caught up with me and we made quick time. Before we knew it we were passing George Maggs’ cottage. He must have seen us coming because without any warning, a water bomb splattered at my feet then another and another. Two more flew at me. One exploded on my shoulder, soaking my coat and splashing my face. The other missed by a whisker. Maggot stood arms folded, in the middle of an open upstairs window, smirking all over his face.

“Feeling a bit wet are we?” he shouted. He let out a loud guffaw and gave us the big thumbs up.

One nil to Maggot. We sprinted out of range.

“Plenty of holiday time to get him back,” grinned Bertie.

For ten more minutes or so I stomped ahead, desperately thinking of how to get revenge.

Bertie called from behind. “Do you even know where you’re going?”

“Of course I do. That’s where I lost sight of him,” I said, pointing to a clump of trees in the distance. “I’ve got a map. We should be okay.”

“Should be?”

Bertie wanted me to be sure but I couldn’t be one hundred percent. However, I *was* sure we could find our way to the path where I saw the mystery man. We were on his trail. I imagined we were pirates seeking out buried treasure.

It took us just under an hour to reach the place that I had observed with the *Jason*. It was still chilly and the breeze was brisk. Despite the cold, the place was alive with the chirping and whistling of bird song. Butterflies flitted past every now and then, along with annoying tiny flies that always made a dart for my mouth.

Eventually, we neared the woodland where I had lost sight of the stranger.

All of a sudden I started to get some 'what if' thoughts - what *if* the man was hiding something from the police? What *if* he's still in the area and he's dangerous? What *if* he sees us? Danger danced into my thinking.

I paused for a moment, took out my tiny space rock and remembered the surge of courage that brought Rat Face to his knees. I needed more of that. For a few seconds I squeezed my lucky rock before pushing it back into my pocket and shouting to Bertie.

"We need to start searching now. It's about here the man turned around." I felt a buzz of excitement.

"You sure this is it?" said Bertie.

"No but we've got to be close."

Bertie threw his hands in the air.

Despite my uncertainty, we got started. We searched like ants desperate for food. Scraping, scrambling and struggling under gorse we were scratched and cut by jagged stones and leaves as sharp as broken glass. Behind and beneath, between and beside we searched, taking hits and bumps from gnarled roots, ragged rocks and solid ground shaped to catch you by surprise.

I turned for a moment and Bertie had disappeared.

"I can't see anything from here."

He was above me, perched on the overhanging branch of a small tree and scanning the ground like a hungry owl.

He jumped and landed with a thud. Inch by inch and heads down we continued the hunt. We didn't notice the change of light. Shades of blue and glinting sunrays gave way to miserable grey. I felt the chill in the air but didn't think about it. Shadows disappeared and large drops of water began to tickle the dry ground, as the black curtain of the storm crept up on us without warning. Bertie was the first to notice.

"Ed, we're going to drown soon."

I ignored him then took off my anorak and squeezed into my red jumper before putting the anorak back on.

“Come on Ed, don’t play the hero.”

“Five minutes more then we jog back.”

“Fine.”

Bertie scowled.

I gave a half-hearted shrug and trudged on. I was getting tired and was almost ready to give up. My weary legs forced their way up yet another slope. Bertie disappeared again behind more gorse. The sound of the rain changed from the gurgling of a stream to the thunder of a waterfall. With aching arms I lifted more low branches. It got harder and harder. I peered behind rocks and tree trunks and struggled to keep my eyes open, as huge globules of water slid down my forehead. I was soaked to the bone and my clothes felt like a new skin. The jumper had doubled in weight. We couldn’t keep going like this. Nature had won. Head down and exhausted I turned to go home. I would have lots of explaining to do.

“Come on Bertie, let’s go,” I shouted.

I ran back down the slope and fell awkwardly at the bottom. Heaving myself up and caked in mud I shouted again.

"Bertie!"

No reply.

I waited, hoping to see Bertie re-appear but no one came. Maybe with the gushing of the rain and the wind roaring through the trees he hadn't heard. I started to make my way back up the slope.

From behind a rocky crag I could just about hear him.

"Over here, look!"

His voice was trembling. He called again, louder and more urgently. I hurried to where I could hear the sound.

Bertie was pale and motionless and his eyes were fixed on a small Hessian sack. The sack was ash brown in colour, a little frayed and tied with string. The knot was tight and made even tighter by being wet. Driven by the pounding rain and the urgency to get home we edged towards our discovery. As we inched closer the rain and wind faded. The storm had passed as quickly as it had arrived. It felt strange, almost magical. Streaming rays of brilliant sunshine now lit up our path and I felt a new strength. In the stillness I could hear my heart. It was a steam train going at full pelt.

However, something was not right. What I saw next was unsettling. Bertie had seen it too. For a few seconds we both froze like the hypnotised prey of a swaying cobra but something kept us going. It was like we were attached to the sack by an invisible thread and the thread was tugging us closer and closer. We had seen something stirring. The sack itself appeared to be moving. No, it was shivering, trembling, shaking. Though it had no voice it was urgently calling us to come closer. We surrendered to the irresistible invitation.

Chapter 6

Drenched, shivering and with legs as heavy as large lumps of wet clay, I edged nearer. I was terrified, but the power of curiosity kept pulling me closer. Bertie got there first. Turning towards me, he signalled with his hand for me to step closer.

"Do you want to open it?" he whispered.

"No you'd better do it," I replied, trying to sound brave.

With trembling hands he lifted the quivering sack. As he felt its weight, he lowered it back down and with some difficulty loosened the wet, tatty string that held it at the top. He pulled it open and as I peered inside I was overpowered by a rampaging army of mixed up feelings. Rage, sorrow, disgust and shock held me in their grip. Bertie didn't move. With one hand he covered his mouth and with the other he made a tight fist.

"Whoever did this isn't human!" he blurted, both hands now clenched.

Before our very eyes were two pups that were left alone to die. I recognised they were Welsh Terriers - the scruffiest and cutest

Welsh terrier puppies you could imagine. My Aunty Pat's Welshie was called Scrap and these two terriers were mini versions of him. Gripping the sack and trying to stay calm I continued to peer inside. These poor little pups shivered out of control. They were trembling with fear and had no strength to climb out of the sack. Helpless and exhausted they peered at us. They looked like gingerbread and black shoe polish all wrapped up in fur. Their long whiskery faces, shoulder and legs were the gingerbread and the rest was the black shoe polish. Their tails were curled over their backs and the fluffy ginger tufts half covered their piercing eyes. The hair on their chins hung down to form a short beard. One pup tried to growl but it sounded more like a whimper. The other gazed, unable to make any kind of noise.

For an instant I turned my gaze from them and hoped that when I looked again I would wake up from this nightmare. Deep down I knew the right thing to do was take them home but something like a dark shadow inside me seemed to be fighting it. More sinister thoughts began to form in my head. I panicked.

“Tie the sack and leave them. They’ll die in no time. We can’t take them home.” My thoughts shot out of my mouth like a poison dart.

Bertie glared at me like I was from a different planet.

“It’s for the best. We won’t be able to keep them,” I murmured, turning away again. “They’re almost dead anyway.”

“You’re joking aren’t you?” Gone was the stare, replaced by a bewildered glare.

I shrugged my shoulders and Bertie’s glare became a raging scowl.

“Coward. Rat Face has more guts than you!”

Still feeling numb I ignored his comment, stepped back and turned to go, hoping Bertie would do the dirty work.

Before I could go one step further he seized my right arm. Locked in his furious grip he dragged me back and shoved my head towards the top of the sack forcing me to think again.

“Look at them. Look at them!”

He held me so hard I couldn't budge.

"You'll never live with yourself. It'll be your horrible secret and I want no part of it."

Ashamed, I looked at the two pitiful pups. They stared back defenceless, longing for care and friendship. In an instant I came to my senses.

"You're right." Tears dribbled down both cheeks.

"Of course I'm right. Now get moving."

What was I thinking? It made me worse than the stranger. Why would *anyone* want to abandon these loveable little rogues who were now balanced on the edge of life? With no time to lose we sprang into action. These cute little pups needed all the care we could give them. They were at most a few weeks old. I held the sack and Bertie sat down and lifted them carefully, one at a time, onto his lap. One tried to jump down, the other lay there exhausted. The brightness had faded from his eyes.

Bertie turned pale.

"I'm not sure this one's going to make it."

I tried to convince myself he was wrong.

"They'll both be fine."

We worked as a team. I took out my bottle of water and Bertie poured some into my cupped hands. One little Welshie didn't need any persuading to drink. With great gusto he lapped up the water, splashing Bertie and I in the process. He came back for more – twice! I broke up my now soggy cheese and tomato sandwich. To begin with he didn't want to eat, but as he sniffed and licked he soon changed his mind and gulped it all down. He made no effort to wriggle free and snuggled up to me as I took him off Bertie's lap and brought him close. His cute black nose was cold and wet against the back of my hand.

The other poor little pup took a few sips of water but that was it. Still shocked, we lowered both shivering pups back into my rucksack.

Our new found friends were in great danger. We needed to get them home in a hurry.

What evil monster could even think to throw away precious lives like this? It was a vile thing to do. I wondered if there were other pups like them. However, these little heroes were now our main concern.

The rucksack was small and one tiny terrier's cute little face poked out of the top. We headed back home, somehow finding the energy to begin our return.

"What you gonna call them? Do you know anything about Welsh Terriers? What will your parents think?"

Bertie fired questions like a machine gun spraying bullets.

As my thoughts raced I wondered if the pups would even make it. When I stopped to check, they were both still shivering out of control.

"My Aunty Pat has a Welsh terrier called Scrap. I used to see Scrap a lot until Aunty Pat moved to Scotland a couple of years ago. Welsh terriers are super little dogs. They're clever and loyal."

I remembered how amusing it was going on walks with Scrap. I hoped I could eventually do the same with these little Welshies.

“C’mon, what about their names?” quizzed Bertie again.

“Moondust and Meteor” I blurted. Where those names came from I have no idea. Until then I’d only thought of boring ones like ‘Red’, ‘Growler’ and ‘Scruff.’

The more I thought about Moondust and Meteor, the more I liked the names. They were just right, I had no doubt.

Although it started okay, the hike home became more exhausting with every step. My trainers were filled with mud and soggy clothes clung to me and weighed me down. Even Bertie struggled. I worried about the poor health of Moondust and Meteor. Maybe we should have left them after all. I rejected that shocking thought as fast as it had arrived.

Bertie and I parted company at the end of the lane. I still couldn’t look him in the eye.

“Sorry about earlier.”

“I never thought you could think like that.”

“I don’t know what I was thinking.”

"Thinking like an idiot, that's what."

He was right. I didn't know what else to say.

"Sorry, anyway."

Bertie gave me a friendly punch on the shoulder. He turned to Moondust and gave him a gentle pat on the head. He did the same to Meteor who was still snuggled up inside the rucksack. Meteor nibbled and licked his hand like he'd known Bertie forever.

"I'm sure you'll take great care of them both."

Bertie already had Bess, a beautiful Golden Labrador.

I could see Dad in the distance clipping the front hedge. Arms folded, he peered over my shoulder. His eyes popped and his mouth dropped towards his growing belly. He threw down his half smoked cigarette.

"Where did you find *him*?"

I explained where we found him and then showed him Meteor in the rucksack. I mentioned nothing about the stranger I had spotted with the telescope and avoided his puzzled stare. Desperate to avoid any more questions, I hurried round the back, took off my boots and stepped inside the kitchen.

"What do *you* want?" asked Mum. Like most mums she seemed to have that special power of knowing when I wanted something.

"Come with me," I said.

I grabbed her wrist and led her out of the kitchen, through the dining room and hallway. I pushed open the front door which Dad had left slightly ajar. He was leaning against the hedge, holding Moondust and Meteor in his giant hands. The pups looked safe and snug. Mum stopped and her mouth fell open.

Moondust had responded well to the food and water. Twice he jumped down from Dad's hands. Eventually Dad left him on the ground and laughed as he whizzed round chasing his tiny tail. He had already grown in energy and strength. Meteor however, struggled to move on his own. The fire of his life was barely lit. There was hardly even a spark. Mum cupped her left hand over her mouth and gazed into the distance. She seemed deep in thought.

Mum's voice broke the short silence.

“Of course you can keep them, dear”.

There was a hint of pity in her voice. I hadn’t even asked if we could keep them.

I punched the air thinking about keeping the two pups but my thoughts turned immediately to Meteor. He was so weak and needed serious care and attention. Mum went indoors to find a box and a warm blanket. Dad brought him inside.

It was then that the unthinkable happened. As he placed Meteor in the box Dad murmured something I didn’t want to hear …“I’m not sure if he’s breathing.”

Chapter 7

Meteor lay there limp and lifeless. His eyes were closed and his head was tucked into his chest. Had he cheated death on the moor only to die in our arms? Surely our rescue wasn't pointless? I felt helpless and all I could do was say 'Please don't die!' over and over in my head. It was the only prayer I could manage.

Moondust was already curled up on mum's new kitchen rug, blissfully unaware of what was happening to his brother.

I reached into my waterlogged pocket and gripped my shooting star. It dug deeply into my skin.

Mum was amazing. Straight away she was on the phone to Alice Carter. Alice was one of Dad's regular clients and a vet at the practise in Ludlow. Fortunately she was at home. Over the phone Alice told mum what to do and Mum rushed back to help Meteor. It was his only hope. The nearest emergency vet was over thirty five minutes drive away in Telford.

Hope flickered like a lonely candle on its last dribble of wax. Meteor was drifting away and death seemed to be closing in. Dad and I were helpless. We looked on as Mum tried with all her might to save Meteor. She was giving him some sort of heart massage. With my right hand I squeezed Dad's giant hand. In my left I continued to grip my space rock. I watched Mum at work. Her brow was furrowed and her eyes were fixed on the task.

"He can't die, he mustn't die. Come on Meteor, pleeeeease come back to us," I pleaded.

Meteor blinked his eyes and the breath of life returned. The heart massage Mum gave Meteor seemed to have worked and Alice Carter came to check him over as soon as she could. I was beginning to like her. She said if Meteor made it through the night then he had a good chance of survival. She would take him to her surgery for a couple of weeks. He would need special attention. Across the living room Moondust was all snuggled up in his box. I looked at him and my heart lifted. He was a survivor. He rolled over onto his back and growled. He blinked and gazed up at me before glancing over to Mum, Dad and Alice. He lifted his little gingerbread paws into the air and I was drawn to tickle his very inviting tummy. He loved it. Then as if to say 'that's enough' our new family member gave a big puppy yawn and turned over again. Alice said Moondust would be fine but she wanted to see him at the surgery on Tuesday. Good news.

After gulping down her second cup of tea, Alice picked up Meteor and made her excuses to go. Just before getting into her car she put her hand on my head.

“Tell me how you found the pups on Tuesday.”

“Sure,” I said.

I wondered if she suspected something.

Moondust dozed off to sleep again, still exhausted from his ordeal. I gazed at him in wonder. He was a very lucky little chap. Stretched out on his side, his front left leg was pointing outwards, like he was showing someone the way. His right leg was tucked under his chin and his paw was curled up almost touching his nose. I imagined he was dreaming about chasing a large rabbit.

The next day, after a trip to church and a delicious Sunday roast, Mum escaped to the garden and Dad relaxed in the lounge, his face buried in the newspaper. *The Shropshire Star* was our local and Dad enjoyed keeping up with events. I was waiting patiently for Dad to finish.

'Knox-Johnson heads home'. I stared at the headline. It looked like Robin Knox-Johnson would be the first man to sail around the world alone. I pictured a tough bearded man dressed head to toe in waterproofs. For a minute I imagined I was in the boat with him with the sails flapping furiously as it rode the crest of a giant wave. Rollercoaster seas surrounded us and thick shadowy thunder skies threatened overhead.

"Do you want to have a look, son?" Dad's voice snapped me out of my watery vision.

"Err, yeah," I said, embarrassed that Dad had caught me dreaming again. He handed me the paper.

I scanned some of the headlines. There were a couple of funny ones:

'*Kangaroo bounces out of local zoo!*'

'*Creamy Crash!*' A story about a milk float* falling on its side.

I thumbed through a few more headlines then turned to the small ads. I was looking for anything to do with dogs. We needed proper equipment for Moondust such as a collar, a lead and toys. Maybe I could find a bargain. My eyes were instantly drawn to one advert near the bottom of the page. I read it again and as I read it for the third and fourth time I tried to convince myself it had nothing to do with poor Moondust and Meteor.

Puppies for sale. Terriers, Labradors and German Shepherds. Longhurst Farm.

Tel. 01286 436219

I struggled with the thought of ignoring the advert, but I had a feeling about it, a gut feeling that wasn't about to let me go.

'Longhurst Farm?' I recognised the name on the advert and planned to make a phone call to ask about buying a pup. I tore the advert from the paper and stuffed it into my pocket.

I wandered into the kitchen and scooped up Moondust. He burrowed his face hard into my chest then turned and nibbled my hand like it was a dog biscuit. I took him outside. He needed a run-around and I needed time to think. As soon as he felt the breeze on his face he scrambled out of my grip, jumped down and whizzed around the garden like a tiny tornado. About twenty minutes and several toilet stops later he calmed down. I had a few moments to wonder about Meteor and hoped with every grain of hope that he was okay. There was no word from Alice.

Scanning the garden, I realised Moondust had made quite a mess. There were chewed plants and chunks of earth everywhere. I brushed off the worst of the mud, picked him up again and took him back inside. He gave me one of those cheeky puppy looks and settled back down to sleep in his basket. Then I realised what the cheeky look was all about. My arm was wet from 'you know what.'

I raced upstairs, washed my hands and arms in warm soapy water and nipped into my bedroom to get a sixpence from my pocket money box. I needed to hurry if I had any chance of spying on Longhurst Farm today. I placed the sixpence into the money tin next to the telephone and suddenly got very nervous about speaking with a stranger. I thought of phoning Bertie instead or Aunty Pat to tell her all about Moondust. Then I remembered Bertie's words: 'Rat

Face has more guts than you,' so I picked up the receiver. My finger fumbled as I started to dial.

"Longhurst Farm…"

There was an awkward pause. I sniffed and almost bit my tongue as I struggled to think of what to say.

"Err, yeah, do you have any puppies for sale?" I babbled. My mouth was dry.

"Yeah. That's what the advert says, dunnit? What kind you lookin' for?

"Terrier," I mumbled. "Can I come and look tomorrow?"

"Come in the morning 'bout half eleven. We're just off Barrow Lane, past Bronson's Garage. Ask for Tony."

"Thanks. Bye."

I let out an enormous sigh and put the phone receiver back into place. I knew exactly where the farm was and I wasn't planning on visiting tomorrow. I was going to *spy* on it TODAY! This could be payback for Moondust and Meteor.

"Who was that?" called Mum. She must have heard me put the phone down.

"Oh, only Bertie."

Longhurst Farm wasn't far away at all. It was no more than a mile or so north of town so I could take the old bridleway and get there in less than half an hour.

"Mum, can I go round Bertie's house?"

"Ask your dad."

I shuffled into the living room, where Dad had his head buried in a book.

"Is it alright if I go to Bertie's house?"

"If your mum thinks it's okay, then I suppose it's alright."

Why did they do this all the time? I called it permission tennis.

Happy that Mum and Dad had finally agreed that I could go, I told them I'd be back before five. The weather seemed set fair. The murky grey clouds of the morning had vanished and there was little chance of the deluge of rain we had yesterday. I put on my white baseball cap, guzzled a large glass of cold water from the tap and headed over to Bertie's, ready to start my new job as a super spy. I crossed my fingers and hoped he would be in. It was a perfect day for a spying mission.

* A small battery powered motor vehicle used to deliver milk to houses.

Chapter 8

I rang the old bell and Bertie's mum appeared at the door. Her wrinkled forehead and pursed lips were not a good sign.

"Not today, Eddie."

Her words didn't surprise me but I didn't give up.

"Please, Mrs Jones."

"I don't think he wants to come out. He's playing with Bess in the garden," she said, "And I think he needs a quiet afternoon after your adventure yesterday."

"Can you just ask him if he wants to come to the park" I said, pleading with my eyes, "It's a lovely afternoon."

She softened.

"Oh, okay dear. I'll go and get him."

My pleading worked a treat.

When Bertie appeared at the door I beckoned him closer.

“I think I know where Moondust and Meteor might have come from,” I said in a hushed voice, “But I’ve told your mum we’re going down the park.”

He stared blankly then frowned.

“Trust me,” I said, “I’ll explain all about it on the way.”

“Er, okay but this’d better be good.”

The frown and stare started to fade and he disappeared to tell his mum.

“Be careful boys,” urged Mrs Jones as we set off.

“How are the Welshies?” asked Bertie straight away.

I peered at the ground and took a deep breath.

“We nearly lost Meteor. We phoned Alice Carter and Mum performed some sort of heart massage. Alice came and she’s taken him back with her. He’ll need proper care for a few weeks. He’s very poorly.”

We made our way up the lane and changing the subject I explained to Bertie all about the advert in the paper and the phone call to Longhurst Farm. His pace quickened and he lowered his voice.

“You know who’s renting it don’t you?”

He paused but I still had no clue.

“Tony Anderson!”

I glanced at Bertie and he was biting his lip. He had turned quite pale.

“I remember Rat Face bragging about it at school one day,” he continued. “He said something about his brother renting a farm to try and make money to pay back a man he owed.”

Bertie was sure Tony Anderson was renting the farm. Straight away, I remembered that when I made the phone call the man said, ‘Ask for Tony.’ Now I felt nothing like a super spy. Tony Anderson was John Anderson’s eldest brother and had served time in prison. The churning in my stomach started again.

“How’s our little Moondust?” asked Bertie, changing the conversation for a moment.

“Hilarious,” I said. “If we put him in the garden, we don’t need a watering can! He has no control at all over his ‘you know what’.”

“Weeeeeeeeeeee!” joked Bertie.

As we made our way along the bridleway, I wondered if we should turn back and go to the park. That was the safer option. We could be heading straight into danger and I wasn’t sure if I could handle danger right now. However, Bertie didn’t seem too bothered and was striding ahead. I jogged to catch up. Overhanging Chestnut and Beech trees gave some shelter from the warming sun. Dark shadows came and went while sunlight danced and twinkled through the trees. The smells were fresh and clean like sunshine after rain. As we rounded a corner George Maggs and his dad were ambling towards us with Porky their overweight dribbling bulldog. When we passed, George sniffed and poked out a bright blue tongue. He’d been sucking on a gobstopper.

“Bombs away,” called Bertie looking over his shoulder, suggesting a revenge attack for the water bombs George had lobbed at us from his house.

I scowled back at George then laughed as he scratched his head and stumbled slightly before plummeting to the ground.

Despite the small distraction, my mind was still racing, thinking about Tony Anderson. Hesitation grew with every uncertain step. The temptation to turn back was huge but we *had* to keep going. This was for Moondust and Meteor. I couldn't let them down.

We were about ten minutes away from the farm when unexpectedly Bertie darted off the path and nipped behind a large beech tree. I followed.

"Look! On the ridge," he said, pointing to the top of the small hill ahead.

I could just about make out the figure of a boy about our size. Bertie had the eyesight of a Harris Hawk.

"It's Rat Face and I think he's crying."

A low sobbing sound carried our way on the breeze.

"Come on, let's go and see what's up," I urged, no longer having any fear of Rat Face. Bertie wasn't convinced.

"What if he wants to get you back for Friday?"

"I think he'll be more scared of us now." I strode forward with Bertie a few steps behind.

We reached the top of the ridge. Rat Face was wrapped up in his little world and only noticed us as our shadows passed over his bowed head. None of us knew quite what to say, so Bertie broke the ice.

"You've got poo on your shoe!"

Rat Face looked up and forced a nervous chuckle.

"What's the matter, John?" asked Bertie.

He explained to us that he'd been to see his brother for the first time in over a year.

"Tony c-cared about me," he said. "None of my other brothers did. I used to love going tree climbing with Tony when I was little. When I banged on the f-farm door and saw Tony I was very 'appy."

Rat Face paused to gather his thoughts. He breathed a big sigh and wiped his eyes.

“At first it was fine. We went mad for a bit playing t-table football. Tony even let me win a couple of games. Then he made me a hot bacon sandwich. I could hear the pups and I wanted to see them. I love p-puppies. But he tried to put me off. Said I should stay in and practise my table football, but I was desperate to see the pups. So Tony showed me around the farm. Now I wish I never did.”

John covered his face and tried to hide the fresh tears. This was a side to John I’d never seen.

“What I saw was like one of them c-concentration camps from the war but this time for puppies. It was ‘orrible. What he’s doing is wrong, taking all them pups to m-make money. ‘I’m trying to pay back what I owe,’ he kept saying. But he shouldn’t treat them little pups like that.”

“Like what?” Bertie and I blurted the words at the same time.

“The place is a mess, filthy, and the kennels aren’t fit for cockroaches,” John continued. “When he f-f-feeds the pups he gives tiny amounts of food - nowhere near enough. He doesn’t care about them. Its money he’s after. What made it even worse was when I saw this tiny little terrier pup. He had 'is nose up against a fence and Tony gave the fence a w-wallop with his foot. The kick sent the p-puppy sprawling to the floor. I felt so sorry for the poor little thing. I ran 'til I reached 'ere. That's when you found me."

Without warning Rat Face stood up and headed back towards the farm. Bertie and I followed.

Rat Face had raced ahead but called back to us, "Come on, I'll show you what I was t-talking about. Whatever you do, don't let Tony s-see you."

At that moment I stopped thinking about him as Rat Face. I felt a bit sorry for him and he seemed to care. Maybe he could be my friend after all. As I caught up with him I told him what happened with Moondust and Meteor and why Bertie and I were headed to the farm.

"Tony would do *anything* to make m-money," said John. "He's desperate to pay back what he owes but this is wrong, so wrong."

At the top of the next rise we stopped and looked down over Longhurst Farm nestled into the side of the hill. It was almost at the bottom of the valley on a gentle slope, with fields to the left, woodland to the right and with the barn, kennels and smaller wooded area behind. The two storey house was built with pale grey granite, had a steep slate roof and ivy clinging to the right hand wall. Red brick chimneys stood proudly at both ends of the roof. It looked peaceful enough but now we knew a more sinister activity was going on.

With John leading the way, we clambered over a low fence out of sight of the house. School bully turned friend – it was hard to believe! We hurried across a small meadow and using the woods as cover, crept round to the back of the farm. As we approached, the foul smell that hit my nose was like a boxer's punch. I knew exactly where the puppies were being kept.

Everything was strangely quiet except for the occasional forlorn howl and pitiful yelp. Keeping low and silent, we came to a fenced-in area and saw the kennels for the first time. I was staggered. They were tiny and old, falling apart. The wood was rotten. As we got nearer, a sad eyed black Labrador pup limped nervously towards the fence.

Something stirred inside me like fire in the belly of a dragon. The scene before me was dreadful. How could anyone keep these precious puppies and not care for them one little bit?

"Quick, hide!" John snapped. The backdoor of the farmhouse had squeaked open.

Bertie and I dived behind a low brick wall. We knelt down on one knee and were ready to make a run for freedom if we had to. I took a deep breath and squeezed as close to the wall as I could. My left hand pressed flat on the concrete floor and my right hand clutched my lucky shooting star for all it was worth. A small spider scuttled past. Anyone looking closely could see the tops of our heads. Bertie's curly brown hair was visible above the top of the wall and part of my baseball cap could be seen, too. I prayed Tony would not look our way. The backdoor of the farmhouse crunched as Tony slammed it behind him. He had spotted John … but had he spotted us?

Chapter 9

Beads of sweat dribbled down my face. I wiped my brow, trying to keep it out of my eyes. I glanced over to Bertie who looked like he was glued to the wall.

"Oi," Tony bellowed, "what are you still doin' 'ere? I thought you'd gone back home."

John had wisely moved away from where Bertie and I were crouched.

"Got bored and wanted to play with some of the pups," said John, moving further away from us.

"Who were you talking to?" asked Tony.

"One of the p-pups," said John.

'Nice answer,' I thought.

"Well you seen too much already. Don't you dare go telling anyone about this part of the farm, or else. If you cost me money you'll be for it. Now get back in the house. I'll call Pa to come and collect you."

John trudged indoors. Tony took another step forward and glanced around. Did he suspect something? I held my breath, closed my eyes and squeezed even tighter up against the wall. A few silent seconds felt like forever until the clomping sound of Tony's heavy footsteps dwindled and the back door clicked shut. I let out a long, low sigh. Bertie crept to where I was still frozen with fear.

"Let's go, NOW!" he whispered.

That snapped me out of my panic and we both jumped up at the same time and ran like crazy for the cover of the woods.

Before long we made it back to the bridle path. At a safe distance, we slowed to a steady walking pace. "John's changed," I said, my heart still thumping.

There was a long pause before Bertie spoke.

"We'll see," he said.

"He cares about the pups," I said, "He wants to be friends with us."

‘Hmm, maybe’ was all Bertie could manage after more hesitation. He said no more.

As we headed home my mind became a thick vegetable soup of questions. Why was Tony Anderson such a cruel monster? How many pups had suffered because of him? How could we save the pups from this dreadful place? Could we really trust John? Bertie didn’t seem so sure.

“We can sneak around the farm again and take pictures,” I said.

Bertie strode ahead and said nothing.

“John could help us by distracting Tony. We could send the pictures to the newspaper. The *Shropshire Star* would love the story. Everyone would know what was going on. Tony would lose everything.”

Bertie stopped and swung round.

“Are you nuts?” he said. “I’m not going back there. It’s too dangerous and we should leave well alone.”

Now it was my turn to glare in disbelief as he turned and marched on ahead. Bertie had given up without a fight.

"We can't leave it as it is. How could we live with *that*?" I shouted after him.

Bertie carried on walking, and then called back.

"Tony Anderson's too dangerous. Even with John on our side he's much too smart for a few kids. Anyway, he won't be there long. Once he's made his money he'll be off."

Bertie's excuses annoyed me. We *had* to do the right thing. I raced up to him and pushed him hard in the back, sending him sprawling to the ground face first. He rolled over wide eyed. I stood over him with my arms folded and gave him the stare of a thousand daggers.

"Tony Anderson won't even know we are there," I bellowed.

Picking himself up Bertie glared back. "How can you be so sure?"

The truth was I didn't know.

"Maybe Alice Carter will help. I have a good feeling about her."

"How do we know she even cares?"

"She cared for Meteor when my mum called."

"That's her job."

Bertie's replies were still irritating me.

"Let's say I've got a hunch about her," I said.

"I'm not going back on 'just a hunch,'" said Bertie. "In fact, I'm never going back there."

That was it. I took another step towards Bertie and got right in his face. We stood nose to nose, forehead to forehead, like two stags spoiling for a fight. I went in for the kill.

"Should we leave them to die?" I bellowed, as I remembered how he had forced *me* to think of Moondust and Meteor.

"I didn't say that," said Bertie in a low voice and stepping back.

"That's what will happen if we do nothing," I replied, still on the attack.

Bertie fell silent. He avoided my glare and looked away into the distance. There was a long and uncomfortable delay. He lowered his head and put his hands in his pockets then shuffled his feet from side to side. As he lifted his head I noticed a tiny sparkle in his eye. Slowly, one of his big cheesy grins spread right across his face.

"You're right, we have to do something," he said.

I relaxed but kept my head high.

"I do like *some* of your ideas," Bertie continued, still grinning, "But we will need to think *everything* through."

We made our way back in silence. All kinds of ideas were popping into my head. The race to rescue the pups was on.

Chapter 10

Murky clouds closed in, blocking the glint of the early evening sun. Long shadows disappeared, light began to fade and the now biting wind made us hurry for the warmth of home. Bertie produced his front door key from his pocket and disappeared into his house. I jogged the rest of the journey, still bewildered by the trip to the farm. I headed around the side of Fern Cottage and Mum's face appeared at the kitchen window. She glared at me but forced a relieved smile. As I opened the back door she threw her arms around me. A moment later we were joined by an elated Moondust with one of Dad's grey woollen socks dangling from his mouth.

"We were just about to come looking for you," said Mum.

At that moment Dad came storming into the kitchen and banged his huge fist on the table. A teaspoon went flying and an old china teacup close to the edge fell to the floor and smashed into pieces. A shocked Moondust leapt out of the way with such force that he slid across the polished floor and flew into the umbrella stand, sending it crashing to the ground.

Mum chuckled but Dad remained stony faced, despite the sock still dangling from Moondust's mouth. I sat down and prepared for the worst.

"You were not at Bertie's at all," he fumed.

I wondered what he knew.

"I phoned Bertie's dad and he told me that you and Bertie had gone down the park. Why did you lie to us?"

"I thought you wouldn't let me go to the park."

It was a weak answer and I dreaded more questions.

"Are you sure there's nothing else you want to tell me?"

I looked out of the window at the darkness closing in. I swallowed hard and then looked back.

"No, that's it," I said, relieved that Mum and Dad thought I had been to the park. They had no idea we had visited Longhurst Farm.

"Trust son. Do you know what trust is?"

"Yes, Dad."

I kept my head down.

"Right son, get up to your room. You need time to do some serious thinking."

That churning was back in my stomach. The right thing to do would be to say where I had *really* been, but I was happy to escape to my room.

Stretched out on my bed for the next couple of hours I cleared my thoughts. I was wrong to trick my parents but not wrong for trying to find out where Moondust and Meteor came from. Somehow I had to get Alice Carter involved. I was convinced she was the key to our mission.

There was a gentle knock on my door.

"You can come down now."

My brief grounding was over. Mum went back downstairs, leaving the tiny tornado to breeze into my room.

Moondust sprang onto my bed, shovelled his ginger head under my pillow and squeezed underneath before popping out the other side. It was funny seeing his tail disappear one side and his head appear the other. Before I could catch him he did it again! And again! Next, he jumped down and grabbed a pair of underpants, which I had left on the floor. The 'pants tug of war' began! His tail wagged flat out and as I tried to grab the pants back he growled and tugged and wrestled as if his life depended on it. Back and fore we pulled, over and over again. In the end, he gave up pulling and I dragged him round and round as he clung with all his might to the pants. We spun like a pair of demented dancers. I twisted round, collapsed and lay exhausted on the carpet. Moondust clambered onto my tummy and gave my face a thoroughly wet licking. I headed downstairs, followed by Moondust, to apologise to Mum and Dad for not telling them about going down the park. That was yet another lie. Still ashamed, I had no idea how long I could keep lying. I took Moondust for a quick run around the garden. He tore around in every direction possible, stopping only to water the plants.

Two days later we bundled him into a cardboard box with a small blanket and headed to Alice Carter's veterinary surgery in Ludlow. It was another beautiful spring morning. The journey wasn't too far but the poor little chap was a bit startled. He yapped and yelped until I lifted him out of the box and held him for the last twenty minutes of the trip. He snuggled up and relaxed when I tickled his tummy. Then without warning he broke wind. Phew! I put him back in his box and covered my nose.

We had an early appointment, so the vet's was almost empty. It smelled a bit like a dentist's surgery mixed with strong salty animal smells. Next to us an elderly lady, dressed entirely in dull shades of brown, sat with her glasses perched on the end of her nose. Resting at her feet in a small cage, she had a bedraggled black and white female cat that shivered and squeezed itself up against the side of the cage. Every now and then it tried to meow but no sound came out. I bent down to glance at the name on the collar round her neck. She was called Cheeky. What a brilliant name! Across the room, a younger blond girl with pigtails and pink ribbons in her hair sat holding her dad's hand. He was carrying an overweight gerbil. Moondust was settled and calm in his box. I wondered how Meteor was but I was a little afraid to ask.

We had only been there a few minutes when the front door creaked open. The stink of cigarette smoke drifted in, followed by a large man with a thin black Labrador pup traipsing behind. I looked up but couldn't see the man's face. The sun poured in through the window behind him leaving a dark outline. He strode across the waiting room with the Labrador hobbling behind and sat down almost opposite us. The pup had a familiar limp and an enormous heat wave of pure panic rushed through my body. It was like my blood was petrol and someone had lit a match in my heart.

I didn't want to look but I forced myself. I gazed down at the man's feet. He was wearing filthy army boots and combat trousers. I kept my head down but let my eyes glance slowly upwards. His legs seemed to go on forever. Next I saw a faded green tee shirt then a familiar leather jacket and cloth cap. One lightning look at the stubble covered face confirmed my worst fears. For a moment, my whole body turned numb as I glanced over again at Tony Anderson and I lost all sensible thought. I looked away, stroked Moondust and tried to think clearly.

I felt Dad's hand on my shoulder.

"What's the matter son? Seen a ghost?"

"I'm fine, Dad."

Nothing could have been further from the truth.

My heart pounded, my fingertips tingled and my left hand began to shake. I took my shooting star from my pocket and gripped it with the shaking hand. Unable to look anywhere in the room, I lowered my head further and stared at the polished wooden floor tiles. The smell of the surgery now made me feel ever so slightly sick. I closed my eyes and began tapping the floor gently with my foot. Taking comfort that Mum and Dad were next to me, I tried to block out any thought of Tony Anderson but it was impossible not to think about the giant bully sitting opposite. I took a few more deep breaths, opened my eyes and glanced at Moondust. He caught my glance and growled playfully. I couldn't help a smile and ever so slowly, normal breathing returned.

After my moment of panic I realised that Tony had no idea who I was. He hadn't spotted me at the farm, so I relaxed and tilted Moondust's box hoping that Tony didn't notice him. When I looked again at Tony I saw that he was too concerned with the sick Labrador to bother with me or any of the others in the room. The pup was sat in front of him panting heavily. Her shoulders drooped slightly and her big brown eyes gazed straight ahead. All the time Tony was mumbling “You’ll be fine, Missy,” and smoothing her down her back. This was not the Tony Anderson I thought I knew.

I looked again at Moondust and thoughts of him and Meteor in that old sack flooded back, as did my anger towards Tony. I glanced at Tony again who was slumped back in his seat. Confused, I wanted to hate him but at that moment I felt uncertainty mixed with some kind of pity. It was a strange recipe. Perhaps he did have a heart after all.

The fifteen minute wait for Alice seemed to take an age. Tony was left on his own in the waiting room when Alice called us. We made our way to her surgery. I stole one more look over at Tony as we strolled past. He cracked a smile and nodded.

“Morning,” he grunted.

I swallowed hard and made myself as tall as I could.

“Morning,” I mumbled back.

Tony turned his attention back to the sad-eyed Labrador sat at his feet.

We stepped inside Alice's room. Everything about her was short. She had short chestnut hair tied back in a very short pony tail. Her short nose made her look part Chinese and she was short in height, extremely short.

"How's Meteor?" I blurted.

"No better, no worse," said Alice in a low tone. "It won't be possible to see him just yet."

I looked over at Mum but she smiled weakly and lifted Moondust from his box.

The tone of Alice's voice changed.

"Hey little chap, what can I do for you?" she said, looking straight at Moondust. It was like she expected an answer.

I told her what I had told my parents about Moondust and Meteor, although somehow I wished I could have told her the whole story there and then. She listened intently.

“You’re a lucky chap,” she said, smiling at Moondust. “I wish your poor little brother was as strong as you.”

The way Alice spoke to him I half expected Moondust to answer back. He peered back at her with his inquisitive look as if he understood every word. Even though he wriggled a bit, Alice seemed to have a calming effect on Moondust. She gave him a thorough examination. Checking his mouth, ears, paws and skin she seemed happy enough but as she studied his eyes she frowned.

“Well, he’s mostly a fine healthy specimen,” she said. “He’ll need all the usual vaccinations, of course.”

It was the ‘mostly’ that stuck out like an oversized rhino’s horn. Nobody spoke, so Alice carried on.

“I’ll need to run a few more tests but I think he might have lens luxation. It’s an eye problem that can be passed on through the family line. There’s nothing to worry about. A little surgery and medication and he’ll be fine.

“How much will the surgery be?” asked Dad.

“We’ll talk about that after the extra tests.”

The more Alice spoke the more I wanted her to help. She was really kind. I thought long and hard about how I could get her involved but my ideas tank remained empty.

'KLUNK! CRASH! SPLOSH!' my train of thought was broken as Moondust tried to leap onto a shelf. Losing his grip, he sent a large box file plummeting to the floor. The shock sent him springing into the air like an excited flea and completely out of control he landed with an almighty splash in the doggy bath. It was a dive worthy of the Olympics. He scrambled out dripping wet and gave himself a major shake, sending mini globules of water spraying in all directions. There were drips flying everywhere and everyone got hit. I got a wet arm, Mum and Alice both had wet faces and poor Dad had a big wet patch in his lap where Moondust had plonked himself down. He held his head high as if he performed that trick every day.

I left the surgery delighted that Moondust was in good health but still severely troubled about Meteor. As I glanced back at Alice the twinkle in her eye gave me a niggling feeling that she knew more about Moondust than she was letting on. We marched back through the near-empty waiting room with a soggy Moondust already settled back in his box. Tony Anderson ignored us as he shuffled past towards Alice's room. Tony was a giant of a man, taller than I had noticed from a distance. Despite seeing him looking after the Labrador, the urge to rescue the pups was stronger than ever.

As we drove home my thoughts flitted from one crazy idea to another, still struggling to come up with any kind of clear plan to rescue the poor pups at Tony's terror farm. I kept coming back to the camera and newspaper idea but realised we desperately needed extra help. It was only a hunch but somehow I thought Alice had to be the key to success. However, when it came to making a meaningful plan that could work I felt clueless, utterly clueless. I had no meaningful plan whatsoever. My heart sunk like a brick in a fish tank as I realised that trying to rescue the pups might be a step too far.

Chapter 11

The following morning a simple thought arrived like a single droplet of light bursting into a black hole. I realised I had missed the obvious answer – the RSPCA. If they saw the mess that Tony Anderson had made they would *have* to close down the puppy farm.

Dad was at work and I waited until Mum had left for the shops in Church Stretton before I phoned Alice Carter. I took a massive risk and blurted out the whole story with Moondust and Meteor. I was surprised when Alice reacted so calmly, until she told me that she was already suspicious of Tony Anderson. She told me he had been to her surgery a few times with different puppies and her instincts told her something was wrong. Then she told me she had already contacted the RSPCA after Bertie and I had found Moondust and Meteor. However, with a shortage of staff and a high workload, they couldn't pay Anderson a visit for at least another two weeks. The dragon fire stirred again. Didn't they realise that even two hours could make the difference to the life of any of those pups? What was the point of having the RSPCA if they were too slow to do their job? I kicked the wall hard with my left foot. Over the phone there was an awkward silence. Alice was the first to speak again.

“Do your parents know anything about what you’ve told me?”

“No, they know nothing. Please don’t say anything,” I begged.

“Don’t worry, leave them to me.”

Alice always seemed to say the right thing. I relaxed.

“So what should we do?” I asked.

“My co-worker, Chris Marshall, could turn up at the farm pretending to buy a dog. Tony has never met him. You and your friends could take photos while Tony is being distracted. I’m sure the newspaper would love to run a story. I’ve also got another phone call to make.”

“Brilliant!” I said, “If that doesn’t shut Anderson down, nothing will.” I felt good. My crazy idea wasn’t so crazy after all. Now it might even work.

“How soon can we do this?”

“Chris is off on Friday so be at the farm by two o’clock unless you hear otherwise.”

Alice hung up straight away like she was some Russian spy. For a moment I sat on the stairs and stared out of the window. We needed a camera, a roll of film and hardest of all we had to keep our secret mission from prying parents.

I couldn't wait to tell Bertie and John. Both were ecstatic with the idea. We agreed not tell our parents anything about the plan. I would ask to borrow Dad's camera pretending to take photos for a 'nature' scrapbook. We would meet at Bertie's just before one o'clock. Being late was not an option. I couldn't wait.

On Wednesday and Thursday I got to know my wonderful little Moondust better, although Meteor was never out of my thoughts. We had great fun chasing round the garden and going for short walks. I had to keep him on his lead as he had no idea when to stop running and come back. The two days were filled with magical moments, like the time we passed Maggot's house and Moondust dug a large hole. Eventually he found a huge bone, probably hidden by Porky the obese Bulldog. It was almost half his body size but he managed to carry it two hundred yards before plonking it on my foot. Later he spotted a buzzard soaring high overhead and made several jumps before realising he wasn't going to reach it. He made a snuffling sound, lifted his nose in the air and walked on.

Getting to Friday seemed to take forever. Since the day we had discovered Tony Anderson's puppy concentration camp, I had dreamed of a rescue mission. As I lay in bed on Thursday evening I began to wonder about our plan. What if we had to make a run for it? Bertie should be fine. He could run almost as fast as he could cycle but I was slower than a three legged tortoise. What would Tony Anderson do if he caught us? He had been to prison and he was a giant. I remembered how John lost his nerve in old Mr Crenshaw's office. Would he do it again? Then I thought about Mum and Dad. They had bought me the most amazing birthday present, taken care of Moondust and tried in vain to save Meteor's life. How did I treat them? By hiding the truth and putting myself and my friends in danger. Part of me wanted to run downstairs and reveal the whole story. The other part of me clung like a limpet to our plan to save the pups.

I must have drifted to sleep as the next thing I felt was something cold, wet and like sandpaper. It was ticklish too! Friday had arrived suddenly with a serious licking from Moondust's tongue. The problem was, he didn't know when to stop. He kept going and going until I dived for cover under the blanket. I giggled and tickled him back before he gave me a friendly nibble on the ear. As I cuddled him, I spoke like he would understand my every word.

"Today we'll try to rescue all your friends. We can't leave them there to suffer."

He stared at me like I was from one of the planets I dreamed of but Friday had arrived with a special Moondust welcome. Operation Anderson was only a few hours away.

Chapter 12

At breakfast Moondust curled up on my lap and nuzzled my tummy, Mum peered blankly whilst tapping the edge of the table with two fingers and Dad again had his head buried in *The Shropshire Star*. Finally, Mum broke the silence.

"So what's this 'nature project'?" she said, as I munched on a thick piece of toast and butter.

"Oh, er, just something Miss Taylor wanted us to do. She wants us to find out about local plants and animals."

"You never mentioned it before."

"No, but I've been busy with other things."

My reply satisfied her curiosity.

Dad was happy for me to take photos for my 'nature project' so I practiced a few photos with Moondust in the garden, with what was left on the old film of the camera. Bertie came over in the morning, so was in a few of the pictures. I couldn't wait to see the close up I took of him and Moondust. Moondust was attacking Bertie and licking his nose. Bertie posed for a picture. His massive cheesy grin filled the lens.

We met after lunch at Bertie's house as planned. Before setting off Bertie produced another camera and dropped it into my rucksack.

"What's wrong with my camera?" I said.

"You never know when it might come in handy," Bertie replied. His familiar smirk spread across his face.

We set off, taking the same route as before. John was quiet and looked a bit pale but I thought nothing of it. Dad's camera was also in the rucksack, along with a bottle of water and Dad's old binoculars.

The ridge where we had first bumped into John was a good place to stop and spy out the farm. We had an excellent view over the field to the yard and towards the menacing old farm building. To the side was the broken down barn, behind which the poor pups were imprisoned. We could also see the road approach from the front.

In the distance I heard the low hum of Chris Marshall's Bedford Van. We waited and soon spotted it approaching along Barrow Lane.

It began to feel like a space rocket countdown. Our rescue plan was almost at 'Blast Off.'

The front door of the car slammed shut. That was the agreed signal for us to move into position, before entering Tony Anderson's nightmare farm. I held out my hand - it was shaking like an excited dog's tail. John, Bertie and I glanced at each other. There was no need to say a word. John rubbed his hands together and looked straight ahead. Bertie took lots of deep breaths and chewed gum. I grasped my shooting star for all I was worth. This was it. This was for the pups.

With Dad's camera at the ready and again led by John we climbed over the fence and crept across the field into the yard. It seemed like John was still trying hard to prove himself. Bertie and I looked left and right. John continued to look straight ahead. We were in the clear. We ducked behind the wall where we had hidden from Tony on Sunday. My hands became sticky and my throat felt dry. We waited, desperately trying not to make a sound. The longer I waited the faster my heart pumped. I glanced at John and Bertie. Both were crouched as low as they could be, chins pressed up against the wall.

Bertie's eyes were narrowed. He chewed on his gum like an old cow. John bit his lip and fixed his gaze straight ahead. A door clicked open and slammed shut. Tony Anderson was on his way out to fetch a pup for Chris. Our time would soon arrive. The photos would reveal what the farm was really like. I turned my right ear in the direction of the house and overheard Tony talking to another person. John raised his eyebrows. He knew exactly who it was.

"That's Jack, my other slimy brother," he whispered. "I can't believe he's involved. He's been living down in Devon."

I swallowed hard and glanced at Bertie who remained grim faced and chewed even harder. Our mission had become twice as dangerous.

"He's probably a supplier," breathed Bertie.

That made perfect sense. The Andersons were running the whole wretched scheme. Jack Anderson was the main supplier of puppies. Tony was selling them on for a higher price.

“He wants a Welshie,” I overheard Tony say. Chris Marshall was going to buy us time to take photos. He and Alice would help us shut down this horrible place. I felt it in my bones.

The Andersons were getting closer and had to pass right by where we were hiding. I could hear the crunch of their footsteps along the gravel path. I held my breath for as long as I could and squeezed even harder against the wall. They were just a few steps away. Terrified, I prayed they wouldn’t spot my rucksack. I had noticed it *might* be visible from where they were stood. Bertie and John were also like statues. Playing musical statues at parties had its benefits. Tony and Jack picked a puppy to show Chris and returned to the house. A few seconds seemed like forever but as the back door at last clicked shut, the Andersons were safely inside. We were in the clear.

Finding it difficult to ignore the awful stench of puppies and the sound of frenzied yelping, we set about our task. Bertie and John kept a look-out as I crept around, camera in hand, taking pictures of the dreadful scenes. This was a place of shame. I zoomed in on the bloated tummies and sad faces of the desperate little pups trapped in this hideous hole. I stepped back, taking pictures from different angles of the cramped conditions and tiny rotting kennels. I clicked away on the camera for all I was worth – I wanted to leave nothing to chance. Operation Anderson was going to plan.

Without warning, Bertie tapped me on the shoulder. I turned to see a wide-eyed look of utter panic on Bertie's face.

"Have you seen John?"

I froze and glanced around in alarm.

Confusion turned to terror as we heard John's unmistakeable voice…

"Over there taking ph- ph-photos!"

My dream of rescuing the puppies was about to turn into a nightmare.

"TRAITOR!" I yelled. Rat Face had returned.

John stood there pointing Tony in our direction. There was no more time for photos.

"Split!" shouted Bertie.

Bertie and I bolted like terrified deer disturbed by the sound of a hunter's footstep. We had rehearsed the move several times even though we hoped it would never happen. Without looking back we ran and ran and ran. This was real and there was no room for mistakes. Heading to the fence in different directions we would meet further up the bridleway. Rat Face had turned traitor. The dragon fire in my belly returned, pumping fresh energy into my legs with every stride. I sprinted with all the strength I could find. Every part of me ached. My lungs were at bursting point.

'Traitor! Traitor! Traitor! Traitor!' I repeated the word over and over in my head with every step as I ran. I knew Tony was somewhere behind me because I heard him clamber over the gate. However, I dared not even glance over my shoulder. Every second counted. Thoughts of Moondust and Meteor and all the other pups released another rush of energy as I strained to escape but I just couldn't go any faster. Fear itself was not enough for me to make my escape, neither was the anger over being betrayed. With every terrified stride I took I could hear Tony Anderson gaining ground. I could feel the thud of his feet on the ground behind me and the sound of panting breath was over my head. My legs got heavier and my heart became weary, like it was melting within me. My mouth dried up and my tongue felt like it was going to stick to the roof of my mouth. Despite having a lead I was no match for Tony. I felt relieved as his giant hand pressed down on my shoulder.

"Gotcha!"

As I turned to face my captor he immediately recognised me.

"You!"

Fear had taken my tongue but I managed to mumble a faint 'yeah' as the puppy punisher marched me back towards the farm.

"We need to talk young man," he said.

That was it. Whatever strength was left inside me dissolved like snow on a barbecue. The battle to rescue the pups had come to a pathetic end. Tony could do what he liked. I couldn't stop the tears so I gave in and let them flow. Fear had now overtaken me. I wanted to be home, home with Moondust racing around the garden. I wanted to be home with Mum and Dad, home with my new telescope gazing at the night sky and dreaming of exploring those distant planets.

My face was wet with tears and as I wiped the tears from my eyes I took my shooting star from my pocket and gripped it in my right hand. With my left hand I held on to the camera for dear life. I jogged ahead of Tony praying he couldn't hear my sobbing. I had to stay brave but under the dark cloud of capture I stumbled and the shooting star spilled from my hand. I desperately glanced around but there was no time to look for it. However, there was enough time to swap the camera I was holding for the one Bertie had slipped into the rucksack. I hurried on, hoping Tony hadn't noticed the swap. As we neared the farmhouse I spotted Bertie going into the kitchen, followed closely by Jack Anderson. My tears had dried on my face in a salty crust but as I slowed to a walk and approached the kitchen door I felt an unusual calm. Tony Anderson said nothing more. Maybe it was the peace before the storm.

Chapter 13

Tony ushered me into the kitchen. He shoved open the door then slammed it shut. Bertie was already slouched in one of the old wooden chairs spread around the large kitchen table. Tears dribbled down his cheeks, which flushed red. I trudged across the kitchen and flopped into the chair opposite. Jack Anderson, who was leaning against the sink, wandered back towards the kitchen door and stood in front of it blocking our exit, arms folded. He smiled menacingly. Jack was lean and his face was craggy, covered with wrinkles and scars. Most of all I noticed his deep set narrow eyes which seemed to soak up everything that was around them. I wouldn't trust him an inch.

The room was quiet and for a moment nobody moved, no one said a word. I noticed every flicker of movement, every sound, every breath.

I couldn't look at Bertie but I sensed his frustration. He would be seething about being caught. Jack Anderson must be a lightning runner. My eyes ignored Tony too, so I glanced around the kitchen trying to keep my mind off what was happening. I needed to gather my thoughts. I gazed at the stone floor, the wood burning stove and the myriad of pots, pans and utensils hanging from the white painted walls. There was a stack of unwashed dishes near the sink and the stench of rotting food came from an open bin. The steady drip of a leaking tap brought some order to the chaos of my mind. Rat Face was nowhere to be seen. I hoped I would never see him again.

Tony Anderson strolled over to me and without uttering a word snatched Bertie's camera from my hand. Before handing it back he removed the roll of film and slipped it into his pocket. I held my breath and hoped he wouldn't look in my rucksack. Moments later, he slumped into one of the chairs at the large kitchen table and broke the uncomfortable silence.

"You boys trying to close me down are you?"

Jack sniggered.

Bertie and I turned our heads and looked at each other but neither of us spoke. However, there was a hint of desperation in Tony Anderson's voice. As I glanced back at Bertie the slight grin told me that he had noticed it too. He sat up like he was ready for action. I stood up in a rush of boldness and seized the moment. My words came tumbling out.

"I was testing my telescope. I saw you carrying the sack in the middle of nowhere. I had to find out more."

"We found the sack, Mr Anderson," said Bertie.

"You left those pups to die," I added.

"Moondust and Meteor," said Bertie

"So it *was* the little Welshie at the vet's," Tony said, staring back at me before looking away.

"I saw the advert in *The Star* then gave you a call," I continued.

Tony Anderson scratched his head and sighed.

"I remember at the time that you sounded quite young but thought no more of it."

Jack's grin had vanished from his face and he nervously bit his lip.

"We came last Sunday to spy on the farm," said Bertie.

"Met John on the way and he was a right mess," I continued. "He couldn't believe how badly you were treating the pups and that you weren't the brother he thought you were."

My confidence was growing.

Tony Anderson sighed heavily again.

Bertie stood up and turned towards Jack.

"John showed us around and we saw your disgusting operation for ourselves."

At that moment the door sprung open and Rat Face slipped in. He bravely stood between Bertie and myself and looked at Tony.

"I thought you c-cared but you don't. All you care about is m-money. You're destroying them dogs, you are."

It was John's turn to go on the attack. I couldn't decide whose side he was on. He carried on glaring at Tony, arms folded.

"I wanted to help my f-friends, to help the pups. I wanted to teach you a lesson."

"But you gave the game away didn't you?" Jack laughed.

"Enough of that," shouted Tony.

He rose to his feet, towering over everyone in the room. John took a step back, Bertie and I leaned back against the table and Jack edged away from the back door. Tony cleared his throat and spoke without any hurry.

"You boys have just speeded up what I should have done weeks ago. I *am* going to close this whole business down."

"You could have said something to me," bellowed Jack, bringing his fist crashing down onto the small table beside him.

There was a short pause before Tony carried on speaking.

"Dumping those poor Welshies, taking Missy and those others to the vets, hearing the cries of those dogs every night and now hearing my little brother is enough for me. There must be a better way to pay off the money I owe."

He bowed his head.

Jack scowled, Bertie grinned and I stood there trembling like a hunted deer. John was pale and barely moved.

“I can’t do this anymore. I don’t care if the RSPCA close me down. I’ve had enough. I need to be as brave as you boys.”

I couldn’t believe my ears. Tony stepped forwards and gave John a giant sized hug. John managed half a smile. Next, Tony took two gigantic strides towards the back door and opened it wide. I glanced at John who shrugged his shoulders before sliding back out of the kitchen.

Tony spoke again.

“Get yourselves home before your parents start worrying.”

Bertie and I didn’t need a second invitation. We bolted out of the door.

I could not believe our turnaround. Like fresh morning rain in the desert, hope had arrived in a most unexpected way. The puppies were going to be fine and we didn’t have to lift a finger.

Chapter 14

We scampered across the yard past the kennels and over the field at the back of the farm towards the bridle path. The relief of my freedom gave me a surge of energy and I ran like I'd never run before. Bertie was only just ahead. As we clambered over the wooden fence I remembered my shooting star. It had to be close by so I pestered Bertie to stop for a few minutes. I was determined to find my lucky shooting star and dropped to the ground on my hands and knees. I began to part the grass and push the small stones around.

"You've got to be kidding, haven't you?"

I ignored Bertie's comment and continued my desperate search. He stayed on his feet, hands on hips, still glaring at me. Suddenly we were startled by the familiar sound of the slam of the farmhouse door. Gazing in the direction of the farmhouse and still crouched down I could see Rat Face running with his head down at great speed in our direction. Forgetting his outburst in the kitchen, I was still fuming that he had betrayed us and secretly hoped he would fall flat on his face. What did he want anyway? Why was he chasing after us?

As John scrambled over the fence Bertie and I slid off the path and ducked down behind a small grass mound. When he jogged past I couldn't resist poking out a leg, sending him sprawling forward with his arms flailing wildly out in front.

"Aaaaaagh!"

"Sorry," I said sarcastically, as he landed with a crunch.

Bertie sniggered.

"Judas John, what are *you* doing here you blubbering coward? You're nothing but a traitor!"

He brushed himself down and stood to his feet, bravely ignoring my anger.

"I had to try and w-warn you," he panted.

"Warn us about what?" Bertie asked.

"Tony's more of a c-conman than you think. He couldn't keep you at the farm but all he *ever* cares about is the m-money. He's going to clear out all the pups today and move them to Jack's place in Devon. He knows the RSPCA will eventually c-catch up with him here."

My mouth fell open. Bertie put his hands to his head and stared at John.

"It's the truth," he continued, "I'm as desperate to save the pups as you. It's just that I was t-terrified of Tony."

"But it's too late now," shouted Bertie, "too late!"

As we stood in stunned silence, the sound of guffaws of laughter drifted in on the breeze. We edged back towards the farm and moved tightly up against the fence. Listening with the strong breeze blowing from the direction of the farm, we could just about hear Jack and Tony. Tony spoke first.

"Ha ha, did you enjoy my performance?"

"That was great acting. You should be in the movies Tony. Maybe you can move to Hollywood," sniggered Jack.

"Yeah, those kids thought I was being serious," boasted Tony. "Now we've bought ourselves enough time to shift those pups.

Come on, let's get a move on. You start cleaning up the kennels. We mustn't leave any trace."

Bertie and I turned and hung our heads. John was right. We looked at each other but said nothing. Our release from the farm had been too easy and victory had never been ours in the first place. We had been cruelly deceived and were now left in the shocking frustration of defeat. Tony had fooled us good and proper. Our one small glimmer of hope was that we had the camera with the pictures of the puppies. Tony had a roll of film but it was empty! However, it was a tiny fragment of optimism – Tony was moving the pups *now* and there was nothing we could do.

The thought of failure crushed me. How could I ever go back to school as if everything was normal? I'd heard about kids running away. Maybe I would take Moondust and Meteor and simply do the same.

With disappointment erupting inside I fell to the floor and hammered my fist onto the ground. It felt good, so I did it a second and third time. Bertie grabbed my arm before I could do it again.

“Stop, that won’t help!” he urged, still gripping my arm.

I caught Bertie’s hard stare then glanced over at John. A single tear trickled slowly down his cheek and before either of us could say anything he turned away, climbed over the fence and trudged back towards the farm. I wanted to go after him but I had been ruthlessly drained of my courage. There was nothing more we could do except retreat from the battle and hope for an invincible knight on a white horse to come charging in on our behalf.

Without uttering a word, Bertie and I left and headed home with the phantom of failure lingering over us.

Chapter 15

Long shadows from the Beech trees cast a murky approach to Bertie's house. Mrs Jones was peering out of the living room window. I wondered how long she had been waiting there, but seeing the stony stare she gave Bertie I decided not to wait to find out. I imagined a similar welcome awaited me at Fern Cottage. So I ambled slowly, weary with the thoughts of those poor pups being herded up and treated just as badly elsewhere. With the full force of my frustration I kicked a stray empty can of Coca Cola, sending it tumbling along the road.

As I rounded the corner, I noticed Alice Carter's small white van parked outside. There was no window welcome and I crept in through the kitchen. Moondust was curled up tightly in his box. One paw was hooked over his nose and his little pink tongue was peeking out slightly. He was fast asleep, dreaming in his own puppy world. Finding this amazing little treasure had triggered my adventure. Daring to rescue him had been the spark that started the fire of the quest for revealing the truth about terrible Tony's puppy farm. I had to do what was right and the fierce hope of seeing all the pups on Tony's farm set free had kept me going. Now the feeble light of that hope had faded sorrowfully into the night. I closed my eyes and rubbed the fresh tears from my cheeks.

As I edged towards the living room all the adults were sat like statues, uncomfortably drinking cups of tea. Mum and Dad were on the sofa and Alice was slouched in an armchair. Mum forced a smile that didn't reach my eyes. Dad and Alice completely avoided my gaze. I was expecting to be hit with the might of Dad's anger but instead, I was greeted with awkward silence. Dad spoke first.

"Sit down son."

"I'm fine, Dad," I replied, leaning up against the door frame.

"No, you need to sit down," he said, using his 'no option' voice.

I chose the rug in front of the fireplace. I crossed my legs and stared again at Mum, Dad and Alice. The awkwardness increased, my tummy tightened and my throat grew dry.

Alice's voice trembled.

"Meteor didn't make it. We did everything we could."

I looked at her and could see the tears in her eyes.

I sprang up, sprinted to my bedroom and lost myself in my heartbreak. It was like my heart was made from glass and it had been smashed with a hammer and shattered into millions of microscopic pieces. Now I hated Tony Anderson. He abandoned Moondust and Meteor, leaving them to die and now he'd got his wish for one of them. Why didn't our plan succeed? Rescuing the pups could never replace Meteor but the thought of Tony carrying on with his disgusting business made me want to punch a hole through the wall. Not even Moondust could heal my pain. The darkness of sorrow wrapped itself around me and held me in its merciless grip. I sobbed myself to sleep.

A loud knocking on my door woke me from my miserable slumber. Bleary eyed and still dazed with sadness I followed Mum downstairs.

"There's someone here you need to meet," she called over her shoulder.

I needed time to think about Meteor but it seemed now wasn't it.

Back in the living room a stranger sat uncomfortably in the only remaining armchair. He was uncomfortable because he was large and the chair was on the small side. The man was bald except for short grey hair either side of his head. He had a thick black moustache and wore round rimmed glasses. He didn't fit well into his navy coloured uniform. The strong scent of cheap aftershave wafted in the air around him.

I plonked myself back on the floor in front of the fireplace, crossing my legs. I wiped my eyes and took several deep breaths.

"Son, this is Trevor Johnson," Dad continued, "A superintendent in the RSPCA."

Trevor Johnson cleared his throat and spoke more like an army officer.

"Eddie, Alice told me all about your discovery and plan. I couldn't let you take the risk, so I ordered my officers to the farm straight away."

I sat up rigidly and raised my eyebrows.

"But your silly officers never arrived at the farm. Tony and Jack are moving those poor pups right at this very moment and my friend John has to watch them do it. They've got away with their sorry business and nothing can get in their way."

"That's where you're wrong," said Trevor calmly, as I listened open mouthed, "You must have only missed my men by fifteen or twenty minutes. They arrived before the Andersons could move the pups. They removed the pups from the kennels and they are now all in the safe care of the RSPCA. The police are involved with Tony and Jack."

I punched the air. Trevor was a strange looking knight but I didn't care. After all that we had been through, I couldn't quite believe what I was hearing. I breathed in deeply again, leaned back and let out a huge breath. At last there was an end to our struggle and it had come in an unexpected way. The pups were safe and terrible Tony would finally pay for his cruelty and blatant law breaking. Our efforts were not in vain. For a moment I was lost for words but as I thought about this incredible result I crumpled in a joyful heap of satisfaction.

In my moment of joy, I jumped up and interrupted Trevor who was about to continue. The whole story of Operation Anderson came pouring out. I hardly paused for breath and I spoke so quickly I'm not sure how much everyone heard.

"Bertie and I got there first. We took pictures but then John panicked and gave the game away. We tried to escape but Tony and Jack were too fast. Tony took what he thought was the camera with the film but I had swapped it for the one Bertie borrowed. They led us back to the farm and conman Tony convinced us he was going to change his ways and close down his puppy farm. After he let us go I stopped to look for my lucky shooting star. John caught us up and reported Tony's plan to shift the pups to Devon. There was nothing more we could do.

Dad shook his head and covered his eyes. Mum's chin shot down almost to the floor.

Trevor, who was 'Mr Calm', spoke again.

"I was hoping my officers would get there first but it sounds like you boys had quite a scare."

Alice chipped in.

"When the local RSPCA office couldn't help straight away I remembered Trevor had spoken at one of my Vet College classes. I knew he lived locally so I took a chance calling his home number."

"Couldn't quite believe what I was hearing," Trevor added, "Tony Anderson was breaking almost every part of the 1911 Protection of Animals Act."

Mum took another sip of her tea and sighed. Dad stared at the ceiling.

"I'm glad *you* are back safely," Mum said.

Before anyone could say another word the tiny tornado tore into the room with another pair of Dad's underpants hanging from his mouth. This time they were navy blue.

Dad groaned. Mum and Alice looked at each other and giggled, while Trevor Johnson struggled to contain the big smirk spreading across his face. I chased Moondust but failed miserably to rescue the underpants which were later condemned to the dustbin.

Slipping back into the kitchen, I picked up the camera and used the last couple of shots on Moondust who had sneaked back into his box.

"Mission accomplished," I blurted, waving the roll of film. But it didn't help the deep pain of losing Meteor.

"We'll get that sent off to the *Star*," said Dad.

"And one of my officers will send a report."

No one argued with Trevor. He excused himself and left. After giving Moondust a quick check, Alice left a short while later.

I was still a bit embarrassed, so to avoid any further questioning from Mum and Dad I phoned Bertie and gave him a rundown of how the RSPCA had finally stepped in to terrible Tony's world. Later, I crept into the living room, snuggled next to Mum and properly said sorry for keeping her and Dad out of the picture.

I wanted the next few days of the Easter holiday to go quickly but it felt like time had almost come to a standstill. When we buried Meteor the next day I squeezed mum's hand harder than I ever had before. Under the dull grey sky mum couldn't hold back the tears and I wept like I did when *Hogan* died. Although Bertie tried to be brave he sobbed too. Alice was there again to lend her support. I liked her a lot.

After a few teary words from mum we slowly trudged inside. No one spoke. In the living room, Moondust was all snuggled up in his box again. I looked at him and my heart lifted. He was a survivor. He rolled over onto his back and growled. He blinked and stared at us. Bertie's face lit up and for a second the massive grin was back. As if he knew we needed cheering up, Moondust lifted his little gingerbread paws into the air and Bertie and I were drawn to tickle his very inviting tummy. He loved it. Then as if to say 'that's enough' our new family member gave a big puppy yawn and turned over again.

The next few days were dreamy - sunny and with wispy clouds skidding through a deep blue sky. They were fun filled days playing and walking with Moondust. On Wednesday night I even tried out the *Jason* and gazed at the moon. It was like a giant pearl shimmering with the silvery reflection of the sun. Yet only one thing filled my mind ... Longhurst Farm. Would the *Shropshire Star* run a story? I really couldn't wait.

Chapter 16

The high pitched buzz of the alarm bell rang in my ear. I threw back the covers and jumped out of bed. Thursday morning had finally arrived and the next edition of our local newspaper, the Shropshire Star, would be zooming its way in white delivery vans to newsagents across the county. I hurried to get ready.

Bertie had cycled down the lane and was waiting outside, whistling '*Old MacDonald had a farm*'. He started singing and changed the words to *'Tony Anderson has a farm, ee i ee i oh. And on that farm he has no pups'*. The words didn't quite fit but it still made me chuckle.

"Come on Frosty, race 'ya," called Bertie.

I took up the challenge but it wasn't long before I fell behind. My cycling skills were terrible. I knew Bertie would win so I deliberately slowed down to save a bit of energy. He waited at the top of the next slope and we glided down the long hill into town.

'Pops' Newsagent was well known to the kids at Edgerton Junior. He sold all the yummy sweets and chocolate bars including my favourites, Aztec Bars and Sherbet Pips.

‘Pops’ and Mrs ‘Pops’ (who was called Val) must have seen us coming. Their two curious and wrinkly old faces appeared at the window right after we leaned our bikes on the wall outside.

Val, who seemed rather surprised by our early arrival, leaned on the counter holding two cups of steaming tea. Pops was straightening a couple of baked bean tins on a shelf.

“Bit early for spending your pocket money on sweets isn’t it?” Pops joked in his heavy country accent.

“A thousand sherbet lemons pleeeeease!” replied Bertie, producing one of his large rubber faced grins. ‘Pops’ chuckled.

“Actually Mr Stephenson, we’d both like a copy of the *Star*,” I said, still huffing and puffing from the earlier bike race.

“They’re not in yet, Eddie… oops, tell a lie.”

As he spoke, the familiar white van with red trimmings pulled up outside. A large pot-bellied man waddled in. He had a bushy ginger beard, wore a blue and white woolly hat and was carrying two heavy looking bundles of newspapers. A half smoked cigarette was casually drooping out of the side of his mouth.

"Mornin' Mr S."

He dumped the bundles of newspapers near the counter and waddled off.

'Pops' pushed the bundles of newspapers against the counter, cut the string and picked the first two copies of 'the Star' off the top. Ignoring the main headline my eyes first focused on the date: Thursday 24th April, 1969.

"That'll be thruppence each."

I handed over a sixpence to 'Pops' and Bertie gave me his thruppence.

"Here's another one for your collection."

I had a tin almost half full of them in my bedroom.

'Pops' and Val gawked in amazement as Bertie and I leaned like two old men against the counter and began thumbing through the latest edition of the *Shropshire Star*. We arrived at the bold headline on page seven at the same time…

'PUPPY RESCUE!'

“Yessssssss!” we both exclaimed.

Underneath the headline and side by side were two of the pictures I had taken. One was of a bedraggled looking litter of Retriever pups, staring helplessly towards the camera. Even though the picture was only black and white you could see that the floor was filthy and that the pups were cramped for space. The other photo showed a fenced off area with the old tiny kennels side by side. Outside one of the kennels was a sad looking pup. She was terribly skinny and cowered in the corner. I remembered her shivering violently and how I wanted to cut the fence to set her free from her torture.

The distressing story beneath the pictures made gripping reading:

The Star can exclusively reveal that a ‘concentration camp’ for puppies has been closed down by the RSPCA right here in south Shropshire. Longhurst Farm outside Church Stretton had been used to keep the pups but the conditions were found to be horrific.

The alarm was raised only days after two local boys discovered a couple of Welsh terrier pups abandoned and left for dead. On seeing a sneakily placed advert in the Star, the boys decided to investigate the farm for themselves. Fortunately, they gained the support of the veterinary practise in Ludlow. The vets already had their suspicions and were only too pleased to help.

One of the vets, Chris Thomas, followed up by going undercover. His visit to the farm was arranged just before the raid by the RSPCA. What he saw was absolutely appalling. In a brief report Mr Thomas noted that...

'... The puppies had bloated stomachs, probably worms too. The poor creatures were dangerously thin. My short observation suggests maltreatment and undernourishment.'

Pictures taken by one of the boys revealed that there were about forty emaciated and hungry pups penned up in the prison.

Swift action was taken against Mr Tony Anderson. His pathetic puppy selling business was immediately closed down and the pups removed to a safe location. Anderson, along with his brother Jack, was later arrested and is now helping police with their enquiries.

Speechless and tingling, I read it again. Bertie still had his face buried in the newspaper. 'Pops had also picked up a copy to read our story. I was glad the Anderson brothers would pay for their terrible treatment of the pups. But then I thought of John. He was desperate for a brother who cared for him and I hoped with all my heart that Tony would change and be the brother that John wanted him to be.

"Right, time to share the good news with everybody," said Bertie getting ready to leave. For a moment he had forgotten that thousands of copies of *the Star* were whizzing their way across the county. The story would soon be breaking news in the living rooms and kitchens across Shropshire and beyond. It had been quite an adventure. Now I felt like I had reached a glorious mountain summit and the view was majestic. For a brief moment I wondered what other mountains I might climb but for now I was king of the world. I couldn't wait to get home. I couldn't wait to see my friends at school.

Chapter 17

Bertie was the first to spot them as he rounded the bend ahead.

"Do you see who I see?" he sang back with glee. His brake squeaked as he slowed to a stop and as I caught up I could see them in the distance. They were unmistakable.

Trudging away from us about a hundred yards ahead was my old friend 'maggot'. Porky the obese Bulldog plodded about three yards behind. Bertie rubbed his hands together.

"It's time for our revenge," he smirked, "Any ideas?"

"Let's not bother, we need to get home." Our battle with Maggot no longer seemed important.

"Come on, this is perfect," Bertie insisted, "Remember the water bombs and his annoying smirk."

I looked around for inspiration.

"Nope, no ideas at all."

Bertie cycled a little further up the road and stopped again next to a grass verge. Straight away I knew what he was thinking. The grass had been freshly cut, was dripping with morning dew and waiting to be dumped all over 'maggot's' long curly hair.

We both grabbed a hefty clump of soggy grass. It was a bit of a balancing job but we sat on the newspapers and managed to guide the bikes with our left hand while holding the grass in our right. Operation 'Maggot' was over in seconds. Bertie approached on 'maggot's' left shoulder and almost came to a stop as he carefully emptied his grass all over 'maggot's' head. Before 'maggot' could react I swooped in and unloaded my clump of grass from the other side.

"Gotcha!"

For a split second I felt bad for doing it but the bewilderment on 'maggot's' face was priceless. We raced away and as I quickly glanced over my shoulder 'Maggot' was rooted to the spot shaking the grass out of his hair and clinging on to Porky's lead.

"I knew we'd get him back for the water bombs," yelled Bertie.

The rest of the journey was over in a finger snap and after resting our bikes on the side wall, we entered round the back of the cottage through the kitchen door. As soon as Moondust spotted us he went ballistic. First he chased his tail. Next, he yapped his little head off and scampered round and round not knowing which one of us to chase. As I sat down he took an almighty leap into my lap and accidentally whacked my chin with his left paw. My face took another licking from his overactive tongue, while Dad put some thick-cut bread under the grill. Everyone was starving. Mum and Dad avidly read the story in the *Star*. Dad was impressed with the pictures and suggested I take up a career in photography. Mum then shared out the hot buttered toast. For me it tasted more delicious than ever – success was sweet. Tony and Jack got what they deserved. Hungrily, we crunched away.

Moondust again jumped in on the action. Attempting to get at my last piece of my toast, he sent the plate on my lap crashing to the floor, shattering the quiet. He looked very pleased with himself and then curled up on the rug in front of the fire. The frown on Mum's face sent me to the kitchen to get the dustpan and brush.

The rest of the Easter holiday sped by and I was soon back at school. In a small community, news spreads like syrup on hot pancakes and everyone seemed to know that Bertie, John and I were the ones involved with the story in the *Star*.

The first day back was bonkers. There was plenty of back slapping from friends. Lots of the little kids stared, smiled and pointed. A new boy even asked Bertie for his autograph. Bertie grinned his cheesy grin and signed the paper 'Michael Mouse'. Basil Scott gave John one of those 'high fives' he had seen on the television and Julie Pearson planted a giant kiss on my cheek as I lined up for lunch. Bertie teased me that I had glowed as red as a prize strawberry.

Miss Taylor let us tell the story of how we had found Moondust, discovered the puppy farm and had a big part to play in the puppy rescue. Bertie's teacher Mrs Sims allowed him to come to my class for the last twenty minutes so we could tell the story together. Everyone longed to meet my tiny tornado. Miss Taylor smiled and nodded. I began to imagine how chaotic the classroom would be with Moondust around.

The day that Moondust finally came in was as crazy as I imagined it would be. Everyone adored him for his mad antics. He soaked up the attention, enjoying every pat and cuddle and licking every face he could get close to. Despite holding him as tightly as I could he escaped my grip twice.

The first time, he leapt onto the Art table sending paintbrushes and several large pots of powder paint tumbling to the floor. Before Miss Taylor could clear up the mess he managed to leave a mini-trail of paw marks in red and blue. He had red and blue powder paint all over him and for some reason he headed for 'maggot' and leapt straight onto his lap, before shaking himself down, leaving 'maggot's' grey jumper and dark trousers covered with the powder paint. It was hard not to laugh. Miss Taylor suggested he go to the cloakroom to clean himself up a bit. When he returned and sat down he forgot that there was powder all over his chair, leaving him with red and blue spots on his wobbly backside.

The second time Moondust wriggled free he scampered round the classroom like a wild piglet then got himself stuck, trying to nose his way into the cupboard under the sink. All you could see was his little bottom sticking out and his stumpy black tail flapping madly like a flag in the wind. Everyone except misery 'maggot' roared with laughter. With Bertie's help Miss Taylor managed to lift the cupboard as I scooped him up again. After the excitement of that day, the summer term slowly rumbled on. The weather turned hot and sticky and the excitement gradually died down. Everything returned to almost normal. At home, Moondust kept everyone on their toes and recovered nicely from his eye operation. More underpants disappeared.

A brilliant surprise awaited me on the first Sunday night of the summer holidays. Reading my space book kept me awake in bed and I must have drifted off to sleep with the light on. The next thing I knew I was startled by a loud knock on my door. Confused, I opened my eyes and gazed up at the light. Dad stood in the doorway. What was going on?

"Get up, there's something you need to see." He disappeared downstairs.

I rubbed the sleep out of my eyes, stretched lazily and took a peek out of the window. It was still pitch black. Dad had got me out of bed in the middle of the night. I checked the time and it was two fifteen. What on earth was he thinking? Suddenly I remembered…

Apollo Eleven was due to land on the moon! Stumbling down the stairs and scooping up a sleeping Moondust I woke him and placed him carefully on my lap. However, he soon returned to sleep and snored his gentle doggy snores. But, *I* was ready to watch a piece of history. This was going to be momentous.

Dad and I were huddled around the small black and white television. The images were grainy and difficult to see but I watched closely as Neil Armstrong appeared from the door of the spacecraft, a rather shadowy, almost mysterious figure. I gazed in wonder as he stepped down the ladder and placed the first human foot on the surface of the moon. I looked at the living room clock. It was five to three.

"*That's one small step for man, one giant leap for mankind.*" Armstrong's voice rang loud and clear.

The words became glued in my mind. History was unfolding before my eyes.

Twenty minutes later, Edwin 'Buzz' Aldrin became the second man on the moon. 'Magnificent desolation', he called it as he joined

Armstrong to collect information and moon dust samples. This was incredible. I was watching live exploration of the moon. This had been part of man's dreams and imaginations throughout history. People from every tribe and nation had written and sang about it. This was the same brilliant shining moon I had seen up close through the *Jason.* Mankind had finally set foot on its surface. Millions around the world were now sharing the moment when dreams came true. Armstrong, Aldrin and Collins would be written into history and NASA had finally got their moon dust. I already had mine.

Later that week, with Moondust curled up at my feet and the sun already sunk deep into the night, I made time to ponder my adventure. I was sat, tummy firmly pressed against the kitchen table. Resting my chin in my hands I leaned forward and closed my eyes. For a few moments I was distracted by the dull ticking of the old grandfather clock. However, it wasn't long before I jumped swiftly onto the boat of my imagination and sailed full pelt into the wild sea of recent memories. And there I stayed for quite some time, riding the waves of mixed emotions – the quarrels with Bertie that tested our friendship, the deep sadness of losing Meteor and the soaring joy of the company of Moondust. Gradually, I drifted back to the safe harbour of real life time and as I thought about the rescued pups snuggling down to sleep in a warm place of safety, my heart burned with the joy of a thousand exploding suns.

13829310R00081

Printed in Great Britain
by Amazon.co.uk, Ltd.,
Marston Gate.